SOL  INVICTUS

The Eye of Ra Book 2

Ben Gartner

Praise for *The Eye of Ra* series

⭐ Gold Recipient, *Mom's Choice Awards Honoring Excellence*

⭐ Silver Medal in Children's Adventure, *2020 International Readers' Favorite Awards*

⭐ Award-winning Finalist, *Next Generation Book Awards*

⭐ 1st Place in both Children's Adventure AND Grades 4th-6th, *2020 TopShelf Awards*

⭐ Grand Prize Winner, *Colorado Author Project*

⭐ 1st Place, *Gertrude Warner Middle Grade Fiction Award*

"An engaging, eventful, history-based fantasy with realistic protagonists and an enjoyable, twist-filled plot." —*Kirkus Reviews* on *The Eye of Ra*

"Once again, Gartner deftly weaves real-life history into a compelling adventure, offering high-stakes, realistic danger and vivid scene-setting." —*Kirkus Reviews* on *Sol Invictus*

"Gartner's middle grade time-travel adventure is a rollicking ride . . . this adventure novel hits the sweet spot. " — *BookLife Reviews by Publishers Weekly* on *The Eye of Ra*

"Gartner has a knack for action and creating compelling historical personalities . . . Middle readers who treasure ancient history with a side of adventure will welcome this fantasy story." —*BookLife Reviews by Publishers Weekly* on *Sol Invictus*

"Gartner's narrative voice complements the book's brisk pacing and heightens its unending action...The book echoes the same adventure-driven narrative of Percy Jackson and the Olympians but with its own Roman twist. However,

Gartner skillfully embellishes a narrow glimpse of history that is typically studied for its grander narrative." —*BookLife Prize, 2021* on *Sol Invictus*

"Ben Gartner has a gift for capturing details of the past and weaving a story that brings the adventure out of history. This series creates a love of history and learning with the wonder and excitement that the siblings find when they travel back in time." —*Readers' Favorite*

"Fun, action-packed read, with a healthy dose of historical facts. Kids will be hooked on this one!" —Adam Perry, author of *The Magicians of Elephant County*

"A heartwarming and fun action adventure novel for the whole family. Full of interesting historical tidbits and fun mishaps, *The Eye of Ra* keeps the pages turning. An excellent read! " —Kerelyn Smith, author of *Mulrox and the Malcognitos*

"With tons of action, humor, excellent character development, and historical details that will make you feel like you've been swept back in time too, this is sure to be a winner for middle grade readers." —Sam Subity, author of *The Last Shadow Warrior*

"*The Eye of Ra* is a delightfully quick and smart magical tour of ancient Egypt, giving middle grade readers an educational survey from the perspective of a modern kid without ever feeling like a lecture." —Jason Henderson, author of *Young Captain Nemo*

"This book was awesome! The book captivated me." —10-year-old book blogger from *Fantastic Books and Where to Find Them*

Also By Ben Gartner

The Eye of Ra
People of the Sun

Copyright © 2021 Ben Gartner

bengartner.com

Published in the United States of America by Crescent Vista Press. Please direct all inquiries to crescentvistapress.com.

Cover by Anne Glenn Design

Library of Congress Control Number: 2020917412

ISBN: 978-1-7341552-3-5 (paperback)
ISBN: 978-1-7341552-5-9 (hardcover)
ISBN: 978-1-7341552-2-8 (ebook)

First Edition, 2021

To my wife, with whom there is never a dull moment.
Thank you for the adventure you bring into our lives.

CHAPTER ONE

Memory Stew

JOHN

John slurped from the spoonful of tilapia barley stew, a special recipe he'd picked up on an unexpected adventure through ancient Egypt. That epic journey had only been a month ago, after fourth grade ended and before they'd moved from Colorado to Maryland, but it was fading like a distant memory. John didn't want to forget, so he made the stew as often as his family could stomach. In part to remind his twelve-year-old sister, Sarah, too.

"Aren't you getting sick of this same soup?" Sarah rolled her eyes, twirling her spoon in the chunky broth.

They'd bonded while dodging cobras and scorpions and figuring out the identity of a tomb robber together, not to mention traveling through time, but Sarah had changed since then, since the move. She'd been acting . . . *different.*

She'd rescued him from a crocodile, for goodness' sake! But lately, when John tried to play with his older sister, she didn't want anything to do with him. Well, most of the time, anyway. Thinking about it now, John's head slumped toward the steaming stew. The pendant of the eye of Ra on a leather strip around his neck, a gift from their ancient Egyptian friend, swung away from his blue Denver Nuggets T-shirt and clattered against the ceramic bowl. John stared at the jade amulet—shaped like an eye with a brow and a line that flowed down into a curlicue end, another line pointing straight down with a knifelike edge—before he tucked it under his collar while glancing at Sarah.

She held his gaze for a moment and John straightened his back. The side of his mouth turned up in a half smile, revealing the lone dimple in his right cheek amid freckle constellations.

"I'm gonna go ride my bike," Sarah grumbled, standing up and dropping her napkin on the table.

"Can I come?" John asked.

"No." She didn't look him in the eye. Then she turned to her parents and jabbed, "Or if we had a dog, maybe I could take it for a walk."

John wanted a puppy too, but Sarah *really* wanted

one and never hesitated at throwing a reminder to her parents.

"Ya gotta eat your dinner." Dad shook both hands, pleading. He was big on them getting their protein.

"At least clear your place," Mom added. Dad tilted his head at Mom, looking disappointed she was letting Sarah get away without finishing her meal.

Sarah sighed loudly and picked up her bowl. After it had been rinsed and lodged in the dishwasher, Dad thanked her.

"I only did it cuz Mom *forced* me," she said.

Dad turned to Mom. "Thanks, honey, for forcing Sarah to do her dish like a respectable human being."

Mom grinned a broad sarcastic smile. "You're welcome, honey. It was my pleasure."

"Ughhh!" Sarah squeaked, her fists at the end of stiff arms as she headed for the back door to the garage. She'd been doing that more often lately too—the high-pitched squeal and a stomp-away.

John watched his parents.

Dad shrugged in exasperation.

Mom's eyebrows raised as she inhaled through her nose. Then she exhaled in a *relax-me* way and turned her attention to John, smiling. "What'd you do this afternoon?"

John took a mouthful of the tilapia fish and shrugged like his dad. "Played some hoops with Roman."

Playing with his best friend in Colorado over FaceTime with a small foam ball and a back-of-the-door hoop wasn't nearly the same as playing together at school on a real court. The fact that he was getting tired of playing over a video call made his heart ache. His conversations with Roman on the phone were already growing shorter. Pretty soon they wouldn't have anything to talk about. At least he still had Sarah. Sort of.

"Oh!" Mom's sudden exclamation roused him from his thoughts.

"What?"

"Roman. That reminds me . . ." Mom looked back at the kitchen counter. She stood and rummaged through some mail, pulling out a glossy flyer. She held it up. On the front was the painting of a bare-chested gladiator with a bright bronze helmet, short sword held high over his head, his sandaled foot on a vanquished opponent lying in the dirt, an arena full of people cheering all around.

"There's a temporary exhibition on the ancient Roman Empire, specifically the frontier region in central Europe, at the natural history museum in DC. We could all take the train in together and check it out this weekend." Mom turned the flyer over and slapped it onto the dining table.

John leaned in and saw pictures of a bright ancient

Roman coin engraved with the bust of an emperor named Constantius, and the statue of a wolf standing while two human babies suckled from below—that image made John giggle.

"Let's do it. Gladiators—what a mind-boggling thing to think about," Dad said, ticking his head back and forth. "Some fought as punishment for a crime or were prisoners of war. But some?" Dad paused, leaning in. "Were *volunteers*. Can you imagine how bad your life had to be to volunteer to kill or be killed in front of a crowd for money? To put your life on the line for entertainment?"

"Like Muhammad Ali?" John asked. He'd done a report last year on the Greatest. *Float like a butterfly, sting like a bee.*

Mom gave a nod like *He has a point.*

"Much more dangerous with swords and spears," Dad said. "Or against lions."

The back door opened and Sarah came in.

"That's terrible," Mom said. "I can't fathom how that behavior was acceptable."

"What?" Sarah sneered, her head cocked to the side. "Are you talking about me?"

"No, sweetheart." Dad chuckled. He stood and moved toward Sarah with his arms out for a hug. "No bike ride? Come here."

"I have a flat."

Sarah let Dad approach, but at the last minute she ducked out of the way so his arms caught only air. She smiled at the evasive move.

Dad looked at John and pointed to Sarah. "I think she'd do okay in the gladiator ring."

John snorted. He looked down into an empty bowl. "Wanna play upstairs, Sarah?"

"No." Though curt, her answer wasn't mean. John still deflated a little, though.

"I'll play, kiddo." Dad put his hand up to John's head but caught himself from ruffling through his hair. John didn't really like that anymore.

After a second of thought, John brightened up. "Wanna wrestle?"

Dad put his hand to his lower back and stretched. "Oy. I'm so old and you're so big now," he said with a smile. "But okay. After I wash the dishes."

"Yesss." John pumped his arm.

"Training for the gladiator games?" Mom asked.

"Why are you guys talking about gladiators?" Sarah asked from the couch in the nearby room. As much as she tried to pull away, her curiosity couldn't keep her far. It wasn't that Sarah was unhappy, she just wanted . . . John didn't know what she wanted. Well, besides a puppy, there was something *else*, was about the best way he could describe it.

"Dad and I want to take you to DC to learn about the

ancient Roman frontier this weekend," Mom said, searching the cupboard for a plastic container.

John could tell by Sarah's perked head that she was interested. But her response didn't match.

"Seriously?" Sarah whined. Her vocabulary lately consisted of a lot of "*seriously?*" John couldn't figure her out. She obviously wanted to go, so why pretend not to?

"It'll be cool," John said half-heartedly. He really did think it would be neat, but he didn't want to commit to his opinion in case Sarah didn't think so too.

"Do I have to?" she asked. "Can I just stay home? By myself?"

John could tell she was practically holding her breath waiting for the answer. She'd been wanting to do this sort of thing more lately too—go places by herself, stay home by herself, whatever . . . *by herself*.

Mom set the leftover container on the counter next to the soup pot, one hand on her hip, and leveled her eyes at Sarah. She smiled, close lipped. "We're going as a family and we want you with us."

"Fine. If you're *forcing* me to."

"Sarah, I asked Dad if he'd wrestle." John beamed.

Sarah understood. "He said yes?"

"Yep."

"Let's talk strategy." She bounded up the stairs, John close on her heels like a new pup.

CHAPTER TWO

A Blast from the Past

SARAH

Arriving at the Smithsonian National Museum of Natural History a good thirty minutes before it opened, Sarah groaned. Their family was over-punctual like that. Even when attending friends' parties where it was assumed you'd arrive a little late, and even though they'd plan for a fashionably late arrival, they'd still show up before everyone else and help the hosts prepare.

The sun had already warmed the air around the National Mall. Sarah scuffled along in her Vans, ripped jean shorts, and green Tony Hawk T-shirt—which contrasted nicely with her flaming red hair.

Mid-summer in DC meant it'd be another hot day.

Sarah squinted and turned her face into the sun. She thought of Ra, the ancient Egyptian sun god, traversing the sky. As the rays dappled her cheeks, she was reminded of the *Aten*, the sun disk that reached out and touched all things. And, in a final violent flash of memory that made her shudder, she saw the tumble of rocks that slid down the mountain and half buried the man with the green eyes: Aten, the tomb robber who had been using the time portal to ferry artifacts from his ancient era to her modern one in exchange for riches. Despite the heat of the sun's rays on her fine skin, Sarah shivered and opened her eyes, pushing the horrible recollection of the landslide from her mind. Aten had been nearly covered but taken away by the police alive.

"It wasn't my fault," she muttered to herself. She looked toward John walking beside their mom, holding her hand. His words from that place echoed as if from the bottom of a deep well. *"It's all your fault!"*

Sarah scowled and shoved her hands into the small pockets of her shorts.

The family meandered toward the nearby butterfly pollinator garden, waiting for the doors to the world-famous museum to open.

The grass and trees had taken a beating the last few weeks with little rain and lots of sun. Each blade bent over as if succumbing to another lashing from the rays.

The leaves hung lethargically from their branches, dangling limp like a dog's tongue.

Mom inhaled a melodramatic whiff of a big purple flower with petals splayed out the size of a grapefruit. "Mmm, don't they smell wonderful?" Her lazy smile made her appear as if she'd just awoken from a cozy dream, or like Alice coming out of Wonderland.

Dad leaned over and stuck his nose up to the petals. "Ah!" he screamed. "Bee!"

He yanked his head back at the same time he pushed the stem away. Needle-sharp thorns lined the branches.

"Yowww!" Dad shook his hand, staring at it as if that would make it better or he couldn't believe what had happened. The bee must have been rattled by the commotion and Dad started swatting with his other hand. Both hands twitching, his head jolting back and forth in spasms, his hair flinging through the air— Sarah couldn't help but giggle.

As soon as she let the chuckle escape her lips, though, Dad froze in his silly posture and grinned at her. "Got ya." He pointed at Sarah and his smile beamed wide enough to show his teeth.

Sarah rolled her eyes and shook her head. "Ugh, whatever." But she was still smiling. Her dad could be such a royal goofball. There was a time she would have joined in happily, but lately she didn't feel like being a goofball as often.

John bounced around Dad like he was riding an imaginary horse, making some weird noise and goggling with his tongue out of his mouth, flapping his head around like Dad had only a moment before, poking fun at him. John was such an easy audience for Dad's antics. Such a sucker for the silly stuff.

"So there was no bee?" Mom asked, her hands held to her chest, her eyes darting around as if a giant alien bee named Bubba was going to pounce on her at any minute.

That gave Dad a laugh. "No bee, honey." He snorted at his own unintentional joke. "No *bee*. *Honey*. Get it?"

Mom groaned. "Clever."

"At least he didn't joke it was a snake," John said.

Mom glared at him. "Don't you even . . ."

John gave a widemouthed goofy laugh and went galloping into a new row. Sarah admired some flowers with creamy-white petals flaring out from bulbous yellow cores laden with rich pollen like a solar corona.

Her parents turned to follow John, leaving Sarah facing the opposite direction. As she spun to join them, out of the corner of her eye she noticed a figure in the shadow near a white alabaster column.

Staring at her?

She did a quick double take and saw the man wore a full-length Egyptian robe with a covering for his head. And he was definitely staring in her direction.

Her parents suddenly seemed a little too far away, so Sarah quickened her pace. She glanced back over her shoulder to catch another glimpse of the man, but he was gone.

Inside the museum, Sarah played it cool. At first, she mostly kept an eye out for other kids her age—especially twelve-year-old boys—but this ancient history stuff actually interested her very much. Not that she'd let anyone know that.

"Eww," she let slip, reading about ancient Roman public bathrooms and the sea sponge on a stick. People would use it to wipe, then dunk it in a bucket of plain or salt water for the next person to use. Ancient TP.

Sarah stuck out her tongue. "Gross."

Out of the corner of her eye, she caught John approaching, so she quickly put her face back to neutral and turned the other direction. The artist's rendering now in front of her was of a boy—probably a little older than her—with icy-blue eyes and long hair the color of a drying carrot, light orange, tied in a knot at one side of his head. Sarah had never seen that style of hairdo before, and for a millisecond she imagined it in her own red hair.

Nope.

"Wonder what happened to his hand," John said, now standing beside her.

The comment tugged at Sarah's curiosity, so she looked down past the boy's bare chest at his right arm. Sure enough, there was only a stump. Secured to his right forearm with tight leather straps, a dull shield. In his left hand, a squat short sword. He wore thick woolen pants and what looked like animal-fur boots. The way he stood on the lichen-covered rock in the picture, with one foot in front of the other, gave him a regal appearance. Sarah's gaze was drawn again to his face, to his pale blue eyes.

"Pretty mountains," John said, obviously trying to get her to say something. She hadn't even noticed the towering peaks in the background of the picture until he pointed them out. John spoke again, reading the caption underneath the painting: "Crocus. A leader of the Germanic people called the Alem—Annie—"

"Al-ah-ma-nee," Sarah said. "Alemanni."

"Alemanni," John repeated. "Who led an uprising against the Roman Empire in the late third century and was responsible for a great deal of destruction throughout Gah—uuu—l."

"Like 'ball,' but 'Gaul,'" Sarah helped.

John looked sidelong at her. "Thanks."

They stood in silence for a moment. Sarah swore the boy in the painting was looking at her. Was that subtle smirk there before?

"Crocus," John continued reading, "ended up siding with the emperor Con—stan—tee—us—"

"Con-stan-shus." Sarah shifted her weight.

"Constantius," John said.

Sarah rolled her eyes, tired of the lessons. She crossed her arms. Her parents were in the hall watching a video at a kiosk. She didn't *not* want to be around her little brother, but nor did she *want* to be around him either. Yes, it was very confusing.

John kept reading out loud, but Sarah started humming to herself and sidled away without him noticing.

CHAPTER THREE

Preparing for the Trip

JOHN

John realized right away that Sarah was leaving, but he chose to ignore her departure and kept reading about Crocus. Interestingly, though originally an enemy of Rome, Crocus influenced the dying Roman emperor Constantius to choose his own son Constantine as the next ruler in 306 CE and—okay, boring. John wanted to read more about the uprising and the "great deal of destruction." And how had the boy lost his hand?

The twinkle of a gold coin caught John's eye. An amateur coin enthusiast, he already held quite a collection of about a hundred coins, including buffalo nickels, wheat pennies, and a liberty dime from 1916. This gold coin in the glass display case had the bust of the emperor Constantius engraved into it with the Latin *redditor lucis aeternae*, which the placard said meant "restorer of the eternal light."

John didn't know what that meant, but it sounded cool.

He spun around, eager to tell his sister about the find. Sarah turned a corner and disappeared. John was about to follow but shot a look back to his parents, who were still engaged in their video. Following Sarah meant he'd be out of sight from their parents, and John knew that was not a wise choice in a busy public place like this. Still, his urge to be with his sister won out and he followed her.

In a side room designed for kids hung racks of costumes. Sarah had slipped on a white sleeveless dress under a sign that said "Stola" and was picking through a pile of shawls labeled "Palla."

On the far wall, John's eye caught the swords, shields, spears, three-pronged pitchforks called tridents, and other weapons and armor of the gladiators. He ran over to a poster showing the various types of fighters and read how each type of gladiator was equipped with a specific set of gear and typically pitted against a specific kind of opponent.

"Wow," he muttered. He never knew such an elaborate system of warrior classes existed for those who fought in the arena.

One particular group caught his attention: The *venatores*. Not technically considered gladiators because they didn't fight humans, the venatores were hunters who battled with animals—lions, bears, tigers, elephants, crocodiles . . . John cringed, remembering the dangerous waters of the Nile and the crocodile that had hunted *him*!

He contemplated whether he'd rather fight an animal like a lion or a crocodile in the ring, or another human. He grimaced at either choice.

Sarah was puzzling with the palla—a long length of fabric—trying to follow the directions to wrap it around her body.

John pulled a tunic made of thick wool over his head. It sort of reminded him of the one he'd worn in ancient Egypt—not very different, actually, but thicker. He grabbed a leather belt upon which hung a scabbard for his short sword. A table with various helmets and headgear offered many choices, and John considered the crown with radiating golden spikes like the rays of the sun. It said this was the type of crown some Roman emperors wore to honor *Sol Invictus*—the "Unconquered Sun," the official sun god and one to whom the soldiers prayed for victory on the battlefield.

"Sun god," John mumbled, subconsciously fingering the eye of Ra pendant under his tunic—Ra being the ancient Egyptian sun god.

"What d'you think?" Sarah turned around in the white stola dress and aquamarine palla hanging over her shoulders. She held a short stubby staff with an eagle at the top—a *scepter*.

John chuckled. He handed Sarah the Sol Invictus crown. "Put this on and you'll look like the Statue of Liberty."

She must have liked the crown's gold bling because she snatched it out of his hand and secured it on her head, holding her neck high with her chin cocked to the side. A floodlight from above shone down on her and glinted off the Sol Invictus crown.

"Wow," John muttered.

"Bow, slave," she said.

Fitting, John thought, and turned back to the table of helmets. He selected a Roman legionary model made of bronze and with a broad plate at the back to protect him from a sword attack to the neck, two strips of steel arcing down over his cheeks.

The round wooden shield painted in red for the god of war, Mars, with a yellow lightning bolt fitted nicely on his arm. The weight of it sent an electric thrill. Fully outfitted in helmet, shield, and sword, his protective armor emboldened him.

John turned to Sarah, weapon raised, ready for the fight.

Sarah struck a regal pose, scanning John up and

down. "I commanded you to bow, slave," she teased.

John scowled and braced himself in an offensive stance, his sword poking out from the top of his shield. "I fight for my freedom!"

"Ooh, fierce," Sarah teased some more, but with a grin.

John lunged at her, ready to slay his opponent. Sarah swung the scepter and parried his thrust, then positioned herself for a duel, one hand behind her back.

As John was about to attack again, a figure suddenly appeared from the shadows behind Sarah. It startled John and knocked him out of focus, but he regained his composure and threw his shield up to fend off Sarah's crashing blow. When he lowered his shield, he saw the figure move toward them—a man dressed in a full-length robe and a hood hiding his face. This distracted John further, but he knew he couldn't let Sarah win this battle to the death.

As he swung his sword, the stranger flipped his hood off and stared at John.

Okay, that was unnerving. John couldn't help but return the man's stare and—

Could it be? Was that—? *No, no, it can't be.*

John tried to voice a warning to his sister, but his brain had temporarily shut down from the complete surprise.

Apparently the shock on his face conveyed the message because Sarah turned toward the man and gasped.

CHAPTER FOUR

The Chosen

SARAH

Sarah instantly recognized those distinct green eyes sunk into that deeply tanned and wrinkled face, the long beard dappled with gray.

Aten.

The man who had been covered in a rockslide and then taken away by police. The tomb robber. The ancient Egyptian time traveler. Memories of their last adventure barraged Sarah's brain like an overwhelming lightning storm. Then her survival reflex blared in alarm.

She swung the scepter toward Aten, and the man recoiled.

"Stay back!" Sarah shouted.

"You must go," Aten said.

"No, *you* must go," Sarah replied, shaking the scepter and moving John behind her. Aten blocked their exit.

"I am but a humble messenger sent by the gods." He put both hands in the air and flicked his eyes toward the ceiling. "Sent by Ra and Khonsu, the gods of the sun and the moon, of light and travel." He looked down to Sarah and John. "The gods have chosen you. And so you must go."

"What does that mean?" John asked. "How did you get out of jail?"

"That doesn't matter," Sarah said. "Let us leave or I'll scream."

Aten grinned. "The gods visited me in my prison cell, where I swore allegiance to them. Yes, I was a thief and a liar, but I have seen the light of Ra and repented. It was they that gave us the power to travel through time. In return for my fealty, they rescued me from that foul place. I will not hurt you, but nor will I fail the gods. You will meet them too someday, when the time is right, and you will see. But for now, you will trust me because I have traveled through the eye of Ra just as you have."

The hairs on Sarah's arm tingled.

"They told me that your trip to Saqqara was merely a test, an introduction, and you succeeded. But now, for your first real mission, your quest—" He paused and leaned in so the light from above shadowed his deep-set green eyes. "You must unite Constantius and Crocus, but beware the one named Alex."

"Huh?" John asked, tugging on Sarah's shirt from behind. "What is he talking about?"

"Obviously nonsense."

"You must travel through time and space again. It is the only way. If you do not, or if you fail to bring Constantius and Crocus together, then the world as you know it is in grave danger." Aten's green eyes bored into them. "Grave danger."

"No, we can't do that," Sarah said, shaking her head, the scepter dropping an inch.

"The gods say that you can, and you will." Aten leaned back upright and put his hands together in his robe.

"Unite Constantius and Crocus?" John asked.

"And beware the one named Alex." Aten nodded.

"Why?" John asked.

"The gods are wise and they command it so."

"This is ridiculous." Sarah inhaled a deep breath and prepared to scream at the top of her lungs.

Just then, a deafening blast made her cringe. She recognized the sound as a fire alarm, but she saw a shudder of panic shake through Aten.

"What was that?" Aten said, fear trembling his

words. He cowered with his hands over his ears.

"Dad!" John shouted. "Mom!"

Sarah knew his cries were drowned out by the alarm. He crouched as if he was preparing to bolt.

Sarah swung the scepter low, trying to knock Aten off balance and out of their way, but she missed.

"Use the pendant!" Aten urged, desperate pleading in his tone. "Hurry!" He started to move toward them. "You must." He shook his hands together. "The gods say it is in your power to save their world, to save yourselves."

Sarah looked past the raving Aten toward the way they'd entered this room, hoping to see their parents. Or anyone. They needed help. They were in a back corner with no other museum visitors, and she couldn't see out into the hallway beyond. This was bad.

Two people passed in front of the doorway in a jog. Sarah screamed out, just at the exact moment another squawk from the fire alarm covered her plea for help. She grunted as the two people didn't even turn to look.

Adrenaline sizzled through Sarah's veins. With hardly even thinking about it, she jabbed the scepter into Aten's ribs. The man groaned.

She used the split moment to jump past Aten.

"No!" Aten cried after her. "You have to go together!" Aten flung his attention back to John and took a step toward him.

Sarah stopped in her tracks. "Leave him alone!" She threw the scepter at Aten but it sailed past him.

John stumbled and fell backward. The eye of Ra pendant dislodged from underneath his shirt.

Aten stopped. "The eye of Ra." He stared at John, transfixed. Another wail from the alarm didn't shake him this time.

Sarah couldn't just leave her brother.

"The pendant has the power," Aten mumbled, reaching toward John with open hands.

Another blast from the alarm jolted Aten out of his dreamy state. The desperation in his green eyes returned. He took another quick step toward John.

And that was when Sarah noticed another shadow approaching.

CHAPTER FIVE

The Power in the Pendant

JOHN

John scrambled backward crab-walk style until he hit the wall. His helmet clattered to the floor, rattling his nerves. The man with the green eyes—the *Egyptian Enigma* the policeman had called him—approached with crooked fingers reaching toward John's chest as if he were going to tear out his heart, a bloodthirsty sneer on his lips.

Huddled against the wall, John clutched the pendant. What could he do?

Where are Mom and Dad?

He took one last look at Aten descending toward him and was about to close his eyes in surrender when he saw a huge man walk briskly into the room past

Sarah and straight toward Aten. John gasped, hope filling his lungs.

Help. This had to be help. Someone to save them.

The huge man's arms were as thick as tree trunks poking out of a tight gray shirt with ripped-off sleeves. One of his ears had a chunk missing so it looked pointed, as if he were elvish.

The giant lifted an ancient ceramic *amphora* jug from one of the Roman displays.

John looked from the giant back at Aten, knowing he was about to get it.

Aten squinted and must have seen the clue in John's face. As the alarm's strobe light flashed, Aten spun. The giant hurled the jug, but Aten dodged the attack. The amphora shattered on the ground.

The strobe light flared.

"Lucas," Aten said, disbelief in his voice. "How'd you—?"

"I followed you right out of that prison. You're the smart one, remember?"

"No—"

"You don't remember that you're the smart one?"

"No, I can't believe—"

"I thought that eye of Ra thing those two talked about sounded like a lot of fun. A real kick in the head, you could say. So I want it."

"You saw the gods?"

"They didn't look like gods to me," Lucas said.

"You saw them." Aten's face lit up. "No—no one believed me. They thought I made the whole thing up." Aten shook his head, backing up from the approaching giant. "You don't understand their power."

"Isn't that why you're here bothering these nice kids?" Lucas said, flipping his hand toward John and Sarah.

John's anxiety was shooting through the roof. Lucas obviously wasn't a friend. But the exit wasn't that far. He could make it. Right?

He looked at Sarah, who was waving him over with clenched teeth and eyes the size of tennis balls.

Lucas grunted and turned his head her way.

Aten took the opportunity and grabbed the nearest thing to him—a wooden shield—and hurled it at Lucas. It clobbered into the back of his skull but barely moved his head. Lucas swung his meaty fist toward Aten, knocking the man in the shoulder. Aten stumbled a few steps before crashing into a windowed display, shattering the glass. The pieces tinkled onto the floor.

The alarm blared. The strobe light flashed.

Aten pulled a dagger from beneath his robes.

"I will protect these children, Lucas. You will not get the pendant." Aten switched the dagger to his other hand. "There are forces greater than anything you can imagine. I must defend the chosen."

The world as you know it is in grave danger. Aten's words echoed in John's mind.

Lucas grabbed another jug and hurled it toward Aten. It missed and shattered on the wall. Aten sliced with his knife, but Lucas blocked it and punched Aten in the gut. The knife dropped, and he doubled over, his face beet red. His knees gave out and Aten fell to the floor, clutching his stomach.

"Run!" Sarah shouted.

John realized immediately she was right. He bolted like a sprinter out of the starting blocks.

Lucas reacted, blocking John's path. John skittered to a stop so fast he fell backward, looking up at the towering man. He basically had no neck and a bald head. His barreled chest cast a strobing shadow on John's upturned face.

"Don't hurt me," John pleaded.

"Give me that necklace or I'll take it." He held out his huge palm.

"Give it to him, Johnny!" Sarah shouted.

One side of Lucas's mouth turned up in a sneer. "She's as smart as the old man." He nodded his chin toward Aten.

Aten had regained himself faster than John thought possible and was running at Lucas with a trident. The three metal prongs looked awfully sharp in the flashing light.

"Enough from you," Lucas said. He dodged Aten's stab, then grabbed the shaft of the weapon and yanked it toward him. Aten lost his balance and came flailing into Lucas's fist. The hammer blow connected on his jaw and cracked his head sideways.

Aten toppled to the floor stiff as a board, unconscious.

Or dead, John thought.

Sarah yelped and covered her mouth. John's throat was dry and he couldn't make a sound, not even a whimper. He suddenly had to go to the bathroom.

John thought his heart rate had been at top speed, but now it skyrocketed. He'd already seen Aten dead once—or so he'd believed. But that was a very different circumstance. That had been from a natural rockslide event, not caused by another human being.

The pendant has the power.

Lucas shoved his hand toward John. "I'll take that necklace now." He held up the fist that had just knocked Aten out.

As if he were in a trance, a calm came over John. Without quite knowing why he was doing what he was about do, he held the pendant in one hand and looked over at Sarah. She had traced the eye of Ra hieroglyph in the cave that took them to ancient Egypt. Was that power somehow in this amulet? If he, not Sarah, traced it this time, would it work for him?

Only one way to find out. John slid his finger along the brow of the eye of Ra.

"John, what are you—" Sarah's eyes widened.

He traced around the almond shape of the eye—

"Stop!" Lucas reached forward.

—and down the line with the curlicue finish.

Lucas grabbed at John, but it was too late.

He finished the design by moving his finger down the line with the knifelike edge.

CHAPTER SIX

A Familiar Flash

SARAH

Sarah knew what was coming next, so she closed her eyes. Even through her scrunched eyelids, the flash of white light seemed to singe the nerves in her eyeballs.

Before she opened them again, she first noticed the absence of the blaring fire alarm. It was quiet. And—

The roar of a wild animal made her jump. She blinked her eyes to adjust to the bright light. At her feet, a blur of brown came into focus. Sand.

Seriously? Her mind went straight to Zack and Rich and Ella, the kids they'd met the last time they were in ancient Egypt.

The roar again. It pulled her eyes up and she saw . . . a lion.

Yes, a real live golden-haired lion. In a cage. Near a wall.

Two thin men in tunics and sandals stood alert on either side of the cage. Then she realized that above the wall were stands, like at a stadium—seats full of people. People staring down at *her*. Then a buzz began from the great crowd—murmuring and pointing. She saw their heads darting back and forth as they chittered with each other, never taking their eyes off her.

Sarah followed the rows of people to her left, spinning around until she'd done a full 360. An entire arena full of people all muttering and pointing—at her.

John coughed. "Sarah?"

Well, pointing at her—and John.

"Ha!" The deep bass of a voice startled Sarah, and she didn't understand how she could have missed the massive Lucas kneeling next to her. He was running his fingers through the sand as Sarah had done the first time she unexpectedly ended up in ancient Egypt.

But this wasn't ancient Egypt.

"Where are we, John?" Sarah asked. "What did you do?"

John's hands shook like he was on a bumpy roller coaster. He had the pendant in one hand and with his other finger was trying to retrace the eye of Ra, but he couldn't steady himself enough and kept losing track.

His eyes kept darting up to Lucas within arm's reach, as if the escaped felon would grab for him again at any moment.

Lucas looked at John, then up at Sarah, then around at the crowd. He was obviously stunned speechless. Sarah knew the feeling.

"Let me." Sarah crouched down quickly next to John. They inched a little farther away from Lucas, and Sarah grabbed the necklace.

A foreign voice from afar announced, "You three! Come!"

"What?" Sarah asked under her breath, moving her attention to the source of the demand. At the front row, in a shaded box all to himself—while the other spectators mashed together behind him—stood a man dressed in a deep purple robe. He wore a golden string of leaves on his head almost like a headband.

No, not a headband. A crown.

The gravity of their situation sank in.

"Sarah," John said. "Is that—is he—"

She reached up and took off the Sol Invictus crown she'd put on in the playroom, examining it more closely. Then she realized she still had on the stola dress and the palla shawl wrapped over her shoulders. She looked at her other hand, half expecting the scepter to be there too. She let the radiant crown drop into the sand. It sparkled.

John still had on his tunic but had lost the shield, sword, and helmet. He must have dropped them back in the museum when they were being attacked.

Sarah looked around at the crowd and realized that they were dressed like she was. Or, more accurately, she was dressed like them. Did that mean that they were actually somewhere—and some-*when*—in the time of the ancient Roman Empire?

"Come. Now!" the man in the box ordered again.

Sarah could understand him clearly, but didn't the Romans speak Latin? Oh, yeah, when they'd arrived in ancient Egypt, she and John could speak and understand the Egyptians' language too. They just couldn't read it.

"Is he the emperor?" Sarah asked John.

John twisted his face and shrugged like, *"How am I supposed to know?"*

Lucas stood suddenly, making Sarah flinch. His massive frame shaded them like a tree.

"Go ahead and make me!" Lucas bellowed in his deep bass. A collective gasp went through the crowd. Despite his size, Sarah thought his tease was pretty mild—something a second grader might say on the playground.

The emperor stood silent for a moment. Then he flicked his wrist and as he sat down said, "Seize them."

"We're not with him!" Sarah yelled. She took a few

steps back from Lucas, scuffling her feet in the sand. John raced after her on all fours.

Sarah now noticed there were a few other people scattered in the ring. They were armed with various weapons and watched her and the middle of the arena with as much interest as the crowd.

Then everyone's attention went to a large double set of wooden doors that burst open with a loud crash. A group of twenty Roman soldiers in formation, all heavily armed and armored, marched at a brisk clip, rectangular red and yellow shields like an advancing wall.

The other combatants all lay down their weapons and put their hands up in surrender. They acted as if this was a usual occurrence and they were following protocol.

"Ha ha!" Lucas shouted, and beat his chest. "Bring it! I love a good fight!" He seemed to have forgotten about the pendant.

The well-trained Roman soldiers didn't falter in their step.

As Sarah shuffled backward, she nearly tripped over John at her ankles.

"Get up." Someone was speaking to John.

Sarah turned to see a boy with a shield on his right arm and a short sword in his left. Why had he not laid down his weapon like the others?

He wore a bronze helmet with a checkered plate covering his face, but based on his height and stature and the way he'd spoken to them, Sarah knew it was a boy, probably about her age, if she had to guess.

His tone seemed kind, but Sarah didn't know if she could trust him.

"Leave him alone," she said, bending down to cover her brother.

"You need my help," the boy said.

"No, we don't," Sarah replied, staring at the helmet.

"Not another one," the boy sighed. "Just get up if you want me to save you."

Sarah scoffed and rolled her eyes. "I'm not a princess. I don't need saving."

The Roman soldiers suddenly halted and formed a line. Spears poked out through notches in the corners of the shields, giving the wall a row of deadly sharp teeth.

"Surrender or we will be forced to attack," a voice commanded from behind the Roman shield wall.

Lucas turned toward one of the unarmed gladiators and ran.

Sarah was taken aback by the big man's cowardice.

"Didn't expect that," said the mystery boy. "Can we go now?"

Lucas gave a frightening snarl at a gladiator, who backed away from the weapons he'd laid down. Lucas confiscated the short sword and shield and turned back toward the Romans.

Sarah hugged her brother tight, a little cocoon of their own.

"Give me the necklace, John," she whispered.

John held it up. Sarah put her finger to the brow and traced around the almond-shaped eye—

CHAPTER SEVEN

Battle in the Arena

JOHN

John's whole body shook. His irregular breathing created a feedback loop of anxious nerves. On one side of him, Lucas was now armed. On the other, a squad or regiment or whatever you call it of Roman soldiers pointed spears at them, and they looked very, very serious. John's worrying spiraled and he couldn't steady himself and—

If only he could trace the eye of Ra again. Why on Earth had he thought tracing it would be a good idea in the first place? What was he thinking?!

Then Sarah asked for him to hand it over. Of course! She would save them. She got them out of ancient Egypt. She'd save them again.

He couldn't get the leather cord over his head, so Sarah leaned in close and put her finger on the pendant. With the loop still around his neck, their foreheads pressed together.

"We're going to get out of here, Johnny," she whispered.

"Get up!" the boy standing over him said again.

Given that he was one of the fighters about to face a lion, John assumed he was a venator and thus wasn't trying to kill them, or the other people in the ring. They were supposed to work together to overcome the lion, right? In fact, this boy had offered to help them. John examined Sarah's face—her single pointed look of determination as she traced the eye. Why was she reluctant to accept this boy's help, to work together?

Sarah finished tracing the almond eye and moved to the line with the curlicue finish while mumbling to herself in some kind of mantra, "Please work, please work, please work."

Before she could complete the circuit, John was yanked away from his sister. Whoever had him was dragging him through the sand on his back away from Sarah. John reached out for her and kicked his feet. Sarah froze for a second, her hands still in the position of tracing the pendant, her eyes watching John stolen away from her. Then she sprang from her crouched position, sand kicking up from her feet as she sped toward John and his captor.

"Let go of him!" she shouted.

John wriggled around enough to see it was the boy venator pulling him. Sarah caught up and latched both hands around John's ankle. With the venator holding him by the collar and Sarah on his ankle, John flew up into the air, stretched between them like a human hammock. Then he crunched back into the sand with a grunt when the boy stopped moving.

"Unless you want to be between them"—the venator pointed at the Roman line—"and that beast." He swung his arm with the shield to point at Lucas hulking toward the Romans. "You come with me."

Lucas bellowed a great war cry and pounded his big feet into the sand, running with full force toward the soldiers like a freight train about to smash into a cliff wall.

John watched in amazement and terror at what might happen next. He wanted to look away, but he couldn't. A Roman spearhead glinted in the rays of the sun.

"Come on, John," Sarah said, holding out her hand. "We're going home."

John heard his sister, but his attention was glued to Lucas about to collide with the soldiers in a few short seconds. Braced for impact, the hardened soldiers didn't look scared at all. How could they not be frightened? They had the numbers, but Lucas was as big as three of them mushed together—which is probably what Lucas was going to do once he reached them.

The venator boy huffed at Sarah. "You're just like her, incredible." He shook his head. "When your friend starts this fight, I'm going to escape through that door. If you don't want to be a slave for the emperor, you'll follow me. Your choice." He glared; at least that's what John imagined he was doing behind his visor.

"He's not our friend," Sarah said, referring to Lucas.

Lucas came within range of the Roman soldiers' spears. He hacked the tip off one with his sword and spun with surprising dexterity to dodge another jabbing thrust, then a third attack nicked across his hip. With a lowered shoulder and his oak-like neck, he smashed into the shields of two men whose helmeted heads only came up to the level of Lucas's chin. Like a raging rhinoceros, Lucas burst through the line, scattering the forces.

The soldiers quickly regrouped from the breach, shouting to each other as they positioned for close-quarters combat, drawing their own swords. The *ssst* sound of weapons being unsheathed added to the suspense of the impending fight.

"Now's our chance," said the venator.

He ran off toward the large wooden double doors.

John watched him go.

"Sarah—" John called.

Sarah scowled toward the emperor, like she was deciding whether to trust him or trust the boy or—John didn't know what. The options were thin.

Lucas swung his sword at the Roman soldiers surrounding him. He kept lunging toward them if they strayed too close into the circle within his reach, snarling like a caged animal.

"Fight me!" Lucas screamed. In response, the lion let out its own fierce roar.

John ran after the venator boy. Anywhere would probably be better than the middle of this arena.

One of the slaves attending the lion made a move to intercept John, but the venator boy growled and shook his sword in a menacing threat. It was enough to scare the unarmed man to back off.

John looked and saw his sister stomping toward him, her fists thrust down at the end of stiff arms. She wasn't running, wasn't looking up, just stalking her way toward the door where John waited impatiently, as if she were invincible. Sometimes she thought she was, John thought, but her scars proved otherwise.

"Hurry!" John cried.

The same lion guardsman who had tried to stop John went to make a move to stop Sarah too, his palms up. "Stop!"

Sarah let loose an angry cry and shook her fists, red hair flaring out around her head like a lion's mane. The man cowered and backed away with a look of surprise.

Okay, *that* made John chuckle. The power of a preteen's frustration was nothing to underestimate.

And with that laugh, John realized he'd taken a deep lungful of air. It felt like the first since they'd arrived in the gladiator ring. He still breathed heavily from the exertion of running through sand and all the excitement, but it was no longer the hyperventilating panic he'd been experiencing moments before. His sister's familiar wrath had grounded him. He laughed again.

The venator boy disappeared into the darkness inside the arched entryway. John moved into the exit, too, while glancing to the battle in the arena.

Roman soldiers lay on the ground all around Lucas, who still begged his remaining opponents for more fight, swinging his sword and running after them. Instead of holding their ground, those standing scattered before he could reach them. But one lucky soldier managed to jab a spear into the back of Lucas's thigh. Lucas gritted his teeth, spun around, and sliced through the air. His sword clanged loudly against the helmet of the Roman soldier who'd stabbed him. The soldier's life was saved because of the protective helmet, but the collision knocked him to the ground, where he lay motionless. Lucas fell to one knee and grabbed at his leg. He spit into the sand. Another spear ripped across his back, and he arched and screamed out, then slumped onto all fours.

John felt his chin quiver. Then he heard Lucas laughing. Laughing in the face of death!

A soldier raised a sword over Lucas's head. John wanted so badly to look away, but he couldn't.

The soldier halted and gestured to the crowd with his sword, then to the emperor and shouted, "Caesar Constantius, how do you rule?"

Constantius. That name rang a bell. He remembered reading about him in the museum, but Aten's words echoed in his mind. *Unite Constantius and Crocus.* Wasn't Crocus the boy in the painting?

The wild audience howled with a primal ferocity. Many of the men had their arms out in front of them, their thumbs turned. A group of women dressed in simple white robes—they looked like ancient nuns or priestesses to John—had their arms out but with the opposite gesture of their thumbs. One of the women even spit into the ring. John didn't know what it all meant, but the sight of the animalistic mob scared him.

The emperor held out his arm with a fist. John sensed that he was about to vote with his thumb— either up or down like the crowd was urging him to do. Was that all it took—Lucas's life in the balance of one turn of the thumb?

His stomach flipped and he thought he might be sick. He'd seen enough. His hand to his mouth, John turned and slipped out of the sun into the darkness.

CHAPTER EIGHT

A Breathing Painting

SARAH

This situation was ridiculous.

How could John have been so—so—*stupid?* Sarah rolled her eyes. She could hear Mom in her head scolding her for using that word. But she didn't care. That was exactly how John had acted.

And to bring Lucas along for the ride!

John's rash action of tracing the eye hadn't helped them; it had made everything worse. Lucas had fought like a rabid dog, but now it looked like he was about to be executed. Even if he was an escaped felon, that wasn't right!

She wanted to think this was all a dream, but having made a similar trip to ancient Egypt, she knew this was all too terribly real. Squeezing her fists tight, she could feel the blood pounding up through her temples.

Why is this happening to me? Why ME? It's not fair!

Sarah wanted to stomp to her room and slam the door so hard it'd rattle the frame (*that* always got a reaction), but she had nowhere to retreat. Despite this wide-open space, she felt oddly cornered, boxed in, unable to make her own choices, forced into something that she didn't want. Boy, that felt familiar. *Ugh.*

Her anger bubbled over, and she let the steam out through her mouth—that's what it felt like as she yelled in frustration. She boiled inside, and if she didn't let it out, she'd explode.

John running after this stranger kid like he would help them would probably just get them in more trouble. Sarah didn't need this new boy's help. She could do it on her own. Just give her a chance to prove herself.

And she didn't need John. She loved her brother, but she didn't *need* him. A vision of her parents flashed in her mind. As much as she loved them too, she didn't need them either. Right? Well, kinda. No, yes, it was time for her to make her own choices, to live her own life. The thought put a little lump in her throat—she missed her sweet mom and goofy dad.

One thing was certain: she didn't need this strange kid practically her age telling her what to do. But she had to get the necklace, and John had the necklace. And John had chased after this kid, so . . .

Once again, her choice was forced. *Ugh!*

She stomped after John, infuriated that he hadn't been able to trace the pendant when they'd first arrived. Such a scaredy-cat.

They could have been back in the museum already, though all she really wanted to do right now was go back to her own room and curl up in bed and pull the covers over her head and shut the world out.

John watched her approach, and she blasted him with daggers from her eyes. He turned and disappeared into the shadow of the door. Good. She didn't want him to look at her.

Nobody look at me.

The large arched gateway leading out of the arena held a deep shadow and she couldn't see inside. Her pace slowed as she approached the threshold.

As Sarah stepped inside, suddenly a hand wrapped itself around her head, and a gross sweaty palm covered her mouth. Her fingers clawed at the hand covering her mouth, and she screamed again, muffled.

She squirmed and tried to bite but couldn't get a piece of the stinky flesh.

"Sarah!" It was John's voice, whispering harshly. But this definitely wasn't John's hand. He wasn't taller than her.

"Be quiet. Your life depends on it." She recognized the stranger boy's voice, his hot breath in her ear. It sounded deeper than it had before, and the threat sent a chill that raised the hairs on her neck.

"It's us, Sarah. Shh." John again.

"There are legionaries coming," the other boy said. "May I remove my hand?"

Sarah nodded, and the hand pulled away. She spit and wiped her lips on her palla.

Turning around, her brother thumped into her with a hug. "That was amazing!"

She didn't return the embrace. Instead, she pushed him away.

John frowned. Ignoring him, Sarah went straight for the pendant. She yanked it toward herself, pulling John closer too.

Quickly she traced the almond-shaped eye, the line with the curlicue finish, and down the line with the knifelike edge.

Nothing.

"What?" she muttered.

"Why didn't it work?" John asked in a little-kid voice that made Sarah want to scream.

She traced the eye of Ra again, more carefully this time, and closed her eyes. Nothing.

"Here they come. Get down." The boy ducked behind a pile of hay in an alcove.

John tugged to go with the boy. Sarah couldn't understand why John kept following this boy. It was infuriating.

"No," Sarah muttered, holding tight to the pendant and leather strap around John's neck, preventing him from moving. She traced the eye of Ra again. Again nothing.

No no no no no.

The boy stood and grabbed Sarah by both shoulders and dragged her into the hiding place. Sarah let him, in a daze. She imagined she'd be back in her own modern time by now. What had gone wrong with the symbol of Ra? What was she missing?

The rhythmic cadence of marching Roman legionaries passed by, their steel clanging as they jogged. The heavy beat of their collective stomping combined with the metallic jostling of their spears, armor, and shields left quite an impression of approaching doom.

Sarah held her breath and put her own hand over her mouth. John had his head ducked into his knees. The other boy watched the army. Though Sarah couldn't see his face through the helmet, she noticed his body tense.

After the army of legionaries passed, the boy spoke. "We're not safe yet, but I know a place we can go."

He dropped his shield, then removed his helmet and

dropped it in the sand, facing away from Sarah. "Fortunately for us, it's Saturnalia. So we have a chance at blending in with the revelers and avoiding suspicion." Then he took off running.

John followed first, then Sarah. She almost tripped on her stola before pulling it up around her thighs so she could really run.

Oil-burning lamps lined the wide passageway, throwing light and shadows dancing over them. Cages lined each side with mysterious dark hints at angry beasts inside. In one, Sarah caught the rounded gray hide of a large animal rump. A rhinoceros lazily turned to watch her pass, chewing on some hay, its pointed horn long and sharp. In another, she saw a hyena pacing in constant motion, its lips in a permanent snarl, drool flopping back and forth.

A high-pitched sawing cat call startled her attention toward the next cage.

Two large eyes reflected the flickering light like fireballs hovering in the dark. A jaguar stepped forward, head low, ears back, its sleek black fur rippling.

John slowed from the boy to run alongside Sarah, who was intentionally not keeping pace while holding her dress up discreetly to run unimpeded.

The next cage looked empty, then Sarah saw a long scaly lump on the ground against the wall, ending in a row of yellowed crocodile teeth. Memories of the Nile River crocodiles swarming for John made her step sideways and bump into her brother.

"Sarah, look." John pointed ahead at the boy's right hand—or where the right hand would normally be. The boy's forearm ended in a stump.

"So?" she replied, not wanting to give John the benefit of a reaction.

"So . . ." John whispered. "The painting?"

Sarah didn't know what John was talking about, and she didn't care. She rolled her eyes and picked up her pace, trying to give John a clue to leave her alone.

Combined with the excitement of the escape and the wild animals, Sarah's heart pounded in her ears. She liked it. The oxygen coursed through her body and made it seem like she could open her eyes wider, like she could sense more of her surroundings, like she was more alive. She inhaled through her nose. The air was musty and slightly dank, but it felt invigorating to breathe deep.

The boy stopped at a junction to take a break. Sunlight streamed in from an exit nearby, and for the first time, Sarah got a good look at the face of the boy she was trying to lose.

His light orange hair the color of a drying carrot was knotted at the side, his eyes an icy pale blue.

"The painting," Sarah mumbled, recognizing what

John had said a few moments ago. "In the museum."

"What?" the boy asked, breathing heavily from the run but not overcome by it.

"That wasn't in the painting of Crocus," John said, pointing at the boy's right cheek. Extending along his jawline, about the height of a quarter, the boy had a tattoo: LIV.

Why does he have a girl's name tattooed on his face? Sarah wondered. Her cheeks flushed at the thought.

"How d'you know my name?" the boy asked.

"Wait," John said. "You're *actually* Crocus?"

The boy squinted at John. "I am. Of the Alemanni. And who are you?"

John smiled like a goofball who'd met a celebrity.

"I—I'm John."

Sarah didn't know what to say.

"Annnnd"—John gestured to his sister—"this is Sarah. My sister. Who usually knows how to talk."

She smiled. "I'm Sarah."

"Hi." Crocus waved awkwardly.

"Hi," Sarah repeated, staring into his mesmerizing pale blue eyes. She reached up and subconsciously twiddled a strand of her red hair.

"Okay," John said, rubbing his hands together. "What now?"

CHAPTER NINE

Time to Party

JOHN

John slapped his hands together again, and Sarah blinked her eyes as if recovering from a shock.

"So," John repeated, "what now?" They'd seen Constantius in the arena. And here was Crocus. Didn't they have to unite these two? But they were obviously enemies—one an emperor, the other a Germanic slave. How were they supposed to unite them? And why? And who was Alex?

Suddenly a loud howl jolted John and he latched on to Sarah.

A man hooted outside the arena at the end of the hall and swung a mug in the air, liquid splashing out.

"Yo Saturnalia!" the man cheered to the crowd.

"What's going on?" John let go of Sarah's arm and cleared his throat as he looked to see if Crocus had caught his embarrassing move.

"It's the beginning of the Romans' Saturnalia celebration," Crocus said. He looked toward the exit and pulled the hood of his cloak over his head. "Come on, let's go."

"Saturn-what?" John asked.

Crocus didn't answer and moved down the hall.

They stopped again at the edge of the tunnel, and John heard some kind of guitar music playing, saw a man blowing fire, a juggler, people dancing and jumping around and generally acting silly.

John smiled. This was his kind of party!

Sarah groaned. "I am *not* going to a party right now." She gestured to her gown and then crossed her arms.

That earned her a confused look from Crocus. "What? No—we're going to use the festival to blend in, okay?"

"Blend in?" Sarah sneered.

"To escape."

Footsteps echoed down the hall.

"I think we should go," John said, tugging on Crocus's cloak.

The boy yanked the fabric out of John's hand, then pulled his hood even lower over his forehead and tucked the edge tighter near his tattoo.

John looked at Sarah, who raised her eyebrows and shrugged in response.

Then Crocus stepped into the light. "Stay close."

"Let's go," John said to his sister.

"Let me try one more time," Sarah said, reaching for the pendant.

As Sarah traced the eye of Ra, John watched Crocus moving farther into the crowd.

"Come on, Sarah, we're going to lose him." He started to inch away.

"Stop moving," she snapped. A second later, she huffed. "It's not working. I guess we can go with him, but—"

"Sarah, we have to go with him," John said. "He's part of our mission, remember?"

She responded with a momentary look of confusion. "Our mission?"

"Unite Constantius and Crocus."

"Can't be." Sarah shook her head.

"But what if it's the key to getting home?" John asked.

A reveler bumped into Sarah from behind, and she yelped in surprise.

John grabbed her from falling over. "He's getting away." He pointed toward Crocus melding into the party. She took off, and John followed her.

"Crocus! Croak!" Sarah yelled. "Hey!"

Someone responded, "Yo Saturnalia!" A few others echoed the refrain as some sort of common celebratory chant.

Sarah ran up to the boy and tapped him on the shoulder.

The hooded figure spun around, startling John. An old man with a large wart on his nose, long gray hairs sticking out of it, scrunched his face. "Who are you?" He squinted at them through milky eyes.

Sarah backed away with palms up. "Sorry, wrong person."

John scanned ahead. Had they lost Crocus? The pace of his breathing increased.

If you fail to bring Constantius and Crocus together, then the world as you know it is in grave danger. Had they failed already?

There were people everywhere, bouncing around, singing and shouting and reveling for whatever this festival was. Laughter erupted to John's right, startling him closer to his sister.

Sarah's head swiveled.

A mask with oversize eyes pounced in front of John, startling him further. The chaos was overwhelming.

"Let's get out of here, Sarah."

Sarah started jogging, holding up her dress with one hand and tugging John after her with the other. "I see him."

A hand gripped John's elbow, holding him back. John screamed and tried to pull away, but the hand had him firmly in its grasp.

"This way." It was Crocus, pointing toward an alley.

John exhaled in relief.

"I knew that," Sarah said, turning abruptly to head in the direction Crocus had indicated.

Crocus tried to hide a half grin. "I know a place we can go where friends will help us. But first, I have to do something."

"Why should we go with you?" Sarah blurted. John gave her a sidelong glance. What was she doing? She seemed to have remembered the mission when he reminded her, so why was she sabotaging it? John just couldn't understand her sometimes. It was frustrating.

Crocus stopped in the alley, which dulled the din of the hubbub in the street. An old tabby cat drank from a pond of brown water that had pooled in the cobblestones.

"Good question," he said. "Why *should* you go with me? Why are you here?"

"I'd like to know that too," John said, seriously wondering how any of this was possible.

"Why are *you* here?" Sarah shot back.

Crocus did that half-grin thing again and replied, "I was captured in a battle against the Roman invaders at Vindonissa and sentenced to *damnatio ad ludum venatorium.*"

John blinked. "I heard your words, but—"

Crocus interrupted. "It's clear you're not from around here."

"Yathink?" Sarah added.

Crocus locked eyes with her for a split second, then continued. "And I think I know who sent you."

"Who *sent* us?" John asked, remembering Aten claiming they'd been chosen by—

"The gods," Crocus said.

John inhaled sharply.

"Well, specifically"—Crocus held up his right arm with missing hand—"Týr sent you to aid me."

"Tee-uhr?" John repeated.

"The warrior god of justice." Crocus sounded wishful, looking to the sky. "Praise him."

John cocked an eye at Sarah.

"Right," Sarah said. "That god. So you have to treat us well, right?"

Crocus laughed. "Of course. You'll help me avenge my father's death and bring justice to the Romans."

John wasn't sure about some revenge plot. He put up his hands. "Whoa, whoa, whoa, I don't know about that—" Sarah pinched him. "Ow!"

"Yep, you nailed it," Sarah said. "We're here to help avenge your father's death after he died in that, um, because of the—"

"After the battle of Lingones at Langres where I lost my hand and was captured."

"After the battle of Lingones, right." Sarah snapped her fingers. "That's what I was about to say. You didn't let me finish. That's what Týr told us, yep."

John caught on. "And we already helped you escape that dam-naughty-oh ad lud-whatever, so that's justice for ya, right? Good old god Týr."

"I could have handled myself against the gladiators." Crocus shrugged. He glanced at Sarah, then cast his eyes down. "They stuck me with the venatores against the animals because I'm technically not an adult yet, but . . ." He trailed off and ran a hand over the back of his neck.

"How old are you?" Sarah asked.

"Halt!"

John looked toward the voice down the alley. Sarah gasped and threw her hand over her mouth.

"Don't move!" A Roman soldier pointed his sword at them, two other armed men behind him.

"Legionaries," Crocus announced. "Time to go!"

John pumped his legs hard as he sprinted alongside Sarah, ahead of Crocus. He focused on the spray of sunshine at the end of the dim alley.

CHAPTER TEN

The House of Mithras

SARAH

All this running, sheesh!

Sarah was getting tired of holding up her long gown. She wished she had a tunic like John. No fair. She did have on jean shorts and her Tony Hawk T-shirt beneath her dress—

She stopped, yanking the stola up around her hips to reveal her shorts.

"Sarah!" John yelled, skidding to a stop. "What're you doing?" He looked nervously back at the approaching Roman legionaries.

Crocus stopped too and glanced away, looking embarrassed at what he saw. Did he think her shorts were her underwear?

"Let's go!" she yelled to Crocus. The boy started running again.

Sarah took a quick right turn and almost knocked over a pail of foul-smelling water. She pressed herself up against the wall next to the bucket and let Crocus and John run past her.

When the Roman legionaries rounded the corner, Sarah tossed the rank water into their faces. They threw their arms up, sputtering in disgust, stumbling blindly. Sarah stuck out her foot and tripped one, who smashed into the other, and they both went crashing into a nearby merchant's stall with the word "Thermopolium" on a banner. The restaurant owner was preparing food for a customer but splattered the stew all over the legionaries instead.

Sarah giggled.

The proprietor shook his hands and shouted at the soldiers.

"Sorry!" Sarah yelled, waving, then ran off.

She turned another couple of corners before she shot a glance back to confirm they'd lost the legionaries. Crocus stopped running but kept moving.

"That was awesome!" John exclaimed. "Nice work." He held up his hand for a high five. Sarah clapped his hand and grinned.

Ahead of them in the distance, rugged snowcapped mountains lined the horizon like razor-sharp teeth piercing the bright blue sky. Those mountains loomed more enormous than the Rockies, where she'd done lots of hiking with her family when they lived in Colorado. She gazed at the beautiful peaks; Maryland didn't have mountains, and she missed them already.

"Where are we?" she muttered to herself. A chill wind made her shiver.

Crocus put his cloak over her shoulders. When she smiled at him, he nodded his head.

"This is the invaders' fort town they call Aventicum," Crocus answered. He turned to the north and chopped his left hand like an ax. "My people are up there, in Alemannia, across the Rhine River." He sighed.

"Then why aren't we going in that direction?" John asked.

"Like I said, there's something I have to do first before I can return to my mother and my tribe." Crocus spun around with a determined look on his face. "We're almost there."

A few more minutes of walking and Crocus slowed his brisk pace, his eyes locked on an expansive two-story house surrounded by a head-high wall painted in a deep maroon and burnt orange. A three-dimensional stone carving inset on the gated archway depicted a man with a knife to the throat of a bull.

"The house with the statue of Mithras. This is it,"

Crocus whispered. He flattened himself against the wall and crept closer to the gate. "Keep watch."

Sarah read a Latin phrase written on the wall. "*Non Nobis Solum*?"

Crocus huffed a breath from his nose.

"*Not for ourselves alone,*" he sneered. "But all the Romans care about is themselves. They—"

"Shhh!" Sarah interrupted. She heard something.

Sarah could feel John's questioning eyes burning into her, but she couldn't handle him right now, so she ignored him and scanned left and right. The worn cobblestones echoed the sound of a pan from the house across the street. But she perked up her ears: the singing came from the other side of the wall. Then the sound of water sloshing, like someone was scrubbing in a pot or a shallow pool back and forth.

Crocus leaned his head around the entryway and peeked inside.

"What're you looking for?" John whispered.

"Quiet," Sarah hissed.

A moment later, Crocus whipped his head back as if recoiling from a flame. "She's alive. Thank Týr." He exhaled a short burst of relief and cocked his head to the sky, his skull thunking against the plaster-and-stone wall.

"Who's alive?" John asked.

"Shh," Sarah snapped.

Crocus whistled like a bird in an intricate warble. The splashing of the water ceased.

He made the same sound again, louder. This time it was returned, echoing his melody perfectly. Crocus beamed a broad smile and whistled again, leaning in toward the gate.

"Crocus? Is that you?" The sound of a girl's whisper. Footsteps slapping against stone. "You're alive!"

Sarah couldn't see in, but two small hands wrapped around the bars of the iron gate.

Crocus put his hand over one of hers on the metal separating them. "I said the same thing about you. Time to leave."

"I can't."

"Now. We need to go." Crocus suddenly seemed more frantic, his head whipping around the area. He yanked on the gate. The metal clanged, but the gate didn't open.

"Shhh! It's locked," the girl said. "But my *dominus* will be leaving tonight to attend a Saturnalia party. That will be the time. Just make sure the gate doesn't latch when he leaves."

Crocus grunted. "Can you get over this wall?"

"I'll walk out the front door. Soon."

"Aurora?" The sound of an older man from within the house. "Come here, please."

"I have to go," the girl whispered. "Tonight, watch

for him to leave and catch the gate." Her hands disappeared from the iron.

"Don't leave my sight," Crocus pleaded, reaching after her through the bars.

"Go!" the girl scolded. Then louder, "Coming, Magistrate!"

Sarah heard the girl's footsteps recede into the house.

"You two stay here," Crocus directed Sarah and John.

"What? Where are you going?" Sarah asked.

John puffed a cheekful of air. "You can't just leave us."

Sarah felt the steam inside her, but suppressed it. The boy she'd been so annoyed with, then who'd grabbed her by the mouth and saved her life from those Roman soldiers, then—those eyes, those beautiful pale blue eyes. She didn't want him to go, but she hated that she might actually need him, whether she liked it or not.

In that moment, Sarah found herself agreeing with John, thinking about Crocus, *You can't just leave us.* She watched Crocus's back as he sprinted around the corner of the house. The whistling steam died inside her before it ever burst out.

CHAPTER ELEVEN

Jailbreak

JOHN

John knew Crocus would come back, wouldn't he? Who was this girl named Aurora, anyway? Why was she so important? Why couldn't he and Sarah take off, maybe head back to the emperor and—

No. The mission.

John took the eye of Ra pendant out of his tunic, as if examining it yet again would yield some new clue. He clenched it in his fist and willed it to give him some sort of sign. He didn't believe Ra was actually a god, but to hedge his bets, he said a few short words of prayer to the solar deity. Then he thought of Sol, the Romans' god of the sun, and tried tossing a few mental pleas in that direction too.

This was silly, asking a star to save him. Weren't Ra and Sol just different names for the same star? He squinted up toward the bright ball of fire hanging in the sky. Considering the sun's power over their lives, he could understand how people came to worship it . . .

"John," Sarah said, putting her hand on top of John's wrapped tightly around the pendant. "We'll find our way home."

"Do you think we have to finish the mission first?"

Sarah laughed and ran a hand through her hair. "I have no idea. It sounds too far-fetched to be true, but maybe. I don't know what to believe anymore."

John gave a half-hearted chuckle, then slid his back down the wall until he thumped to the ground.

"Aw, come on, Johnny." She sat next to him. "We'll figure it out. We always do." She slapped him on the knee.

John looked out toward the gorgeous towering mountains. Despite the circumstances, the view was pretty breathtaking. But he couldn't shake the nagging feeling that Crocus was gone.

"Is he coming back?" John asked.

"Do you know what mountains those are?"

"No idea."

"I think I do," Sarah said, grinning.

"Tell me."

She pointed behind them, away from the mountains. "When Croak told us his tribe is that way, he said north."

"Croak?" John smirked.

"Crocus. Whatever." Then Sarah pointed at the sun to their right. "So that must be west, and it's afternoon right now."

"It was morning when we left the museum," John said.

"Like time travel cares?"

John snorted. "Right."

"Anyway, if the Rhine is north of us, that means we're south of Germany—what Crocus called Alemannia, I think. So maybe we're in Switzerland?"

John squinted at her. "How do you know all this?"

"The map on my wall. Preparing for our family trip to Europe next year?"

"Wow, you're smart."

Sarah chuckled. "So those mountains must be—"

"Unlike any mountains I've ever seen."

"The Alps."

"Wow," John said, leaning his head back. "They're . . ." He trailed off, thinking of the right word. "Magnificent."

Sarah swiveled her head and gave him a second look. *"Magnificent?"*

"What?"

"Since when do you use words like 'magnificent'?"

John shrugged. "Since I saw the Alps, I guess." He chuckled. "No wonder Dad wants to bring us here."

"That looks a little menacing, though, don't you think?" Sarah gestured to the dark clouds frothing in the valley straight ahead.

Just then, the gate rattled, startling them both to their feet. John grabbed Sarah's arm. Sarah was squeezing his hand tightly back.

The gate flung open and Crocus hurried out, pulling a little girl probably younger than John. She had orangey-red hair similar to Crocus's.

"Run!" Crocus barked, tearing off on the stone path away from the villa.

"Again?" John asked, shoulders slumping. This day had already been more exercise than a full week of PE.

"Guards!" shouted the old man from within the courtyard. "After that slave!"

"I guess we're running." Sarah shrugged and took off after Crocus, yanking John along.

They ran down the hill together. As they turned the corner, John looked back to see two guards, swords on their belts, chasing after them.

Crocus jumped into the driver's seat of a farmer's wagon by the side of the road and grabbed the reins of the two horses. "Get in."

"That'd be stealing," John said.

"Yep."

Aurora didn't hesitate and climbed onto the bench next to Crocus. Sarah jumped into the back full of hay and put her hand out to John. He had one foot on the back gate, his hand in Sarah's, when Crocus whipped the leather straps and shouted, "Yah!"

The horses whinnied in surprise and lurched, jerking the wagon forward. John swung sideways, one foot on the tailgate and the other dangling over the ground suddenly rushing below.

"Stop!" The guards had rounded the corner and were waving their arms, but losing ground fast.

"Sarah!" John cried, hanging precariously off the edge as it continued to increase speed. Sarah grabbed his forearm and pulled him up. He landed on top of her.

A laugh burst loud from John, and he rolled over into the soft hay, staring up at the sky and just laughing, anxious giddiness bubbling out from the sudden exhilaration of the escape and nearly falling off the speeding wagon.

The girl in the front seat looked back and giggled at him. She sighed. "I'm Aurora."

John settled down and propped himself on an elbow. "John." He waved.

Sarah introduced herself too.

Aurora suddenly looked like she might cry.

"What's wrong?" John asked.

A tear slipped down her cheek as she turned her head to their driver. "I thought Crocus was dead."

"Not yet," Crocus said, smiling.

They rounded a bend and came out from behind a low hill. Crocus pointed down the stretch of road to a darkly shrouded valley between two enormous peaks of the Alps. "Safety is there."

John gulped. "Really?"

"There's a secret camp. We'll meet up with the other Alemanni on this side of the Rhine." Crocus glanced behind them, then snapped the reins again.

"We're being followed!" Aurora exclaimed.

John spun around. Speeding up the road were the guards from the magistrate's house, standing in a two-wheeled chariot pulled by a fast horse.

Sarah hunkered down next to John. "We need to get Crocus back to Constantius."

John didn't know how to respond, his eyes glued to the chariot gaining on them.

"Use that pitchfork." Crocus pointed to the three-pronged iron farmer's tool bouncing against the side board of the wagon.

The chariot was only yards away. One guard drove while the other raised a spear.

There's no way they're going to throw that at us—

The spear whizzed over John's head and narrowly

missed Crocus. Their cart careened to the right, and the nose of the chariot's horse came up even with the back of their wagon on the left side—John's side. John squirmed away against the headboard. In the chill air, the horse's snorting breaths sent puffy clouds shooting toward John like a dragon's. The guard who'd thrown the spear now held a dagger in his teeth and reached his hands to grab hold of the wagon.

"He's trying to board!" Aurora screamed. She threw something—*an orange?*—at the man, and it bounced off his forehead. It stunned the guard for only a moment, but it bought them a little more time.

"John," Crocus yelled over the noise of the clattering horses on the cobblestone road, "shove that pitchfork into their wheel!"

"What?!" John shouted back. "I can't do that!"

"You have to!" Aurora said.

The guard with the dagger reached out again, this time his hand landing firmly on the edge of the wood. The chariot crashed against the wagon, and John gasped.

"Now!" Crocus yanked back and right on the reins, slowing them down and veering them away from the chariot. The guard held on to the wagon with one hand and was pulled from his vehicle. His legs scraped along the ground, and he cried out, then dropped and rolled away off the road.

"Yeah!" Crocus shouted. But the victory was short-lived. The chariot driver aimed his vehicle at the wagon on a direct collision course. He was trying to run them off the road.

"John! Now!" Crocus barked.

John knew he had to do it. And he had to do it now. Now! His primal survival brain took hold, and he looked over to grab the pitchfork.

But Sarah already had it in her hands. She stood up in the back of the shaking wagon—her years of skateboarding and skiing helping her to maintain balance—and with both hands, she shoved the pitchfork through the air. John, holding his breath, watched it sail over his head and land directly in the middle of the spokes of the chariot wheel.

There was a loud snapping of wood, and the pitchfork's long wooden handle exploded in a shower of splinters.

The chariot kept moving.

The driver smiled and cracked his reins.

As the chariot neared, Sarah fell back into the hay next to John.

Collision imminent.

At the last possible second, the right wheel of the chariot collapsed in on itself, and the carriage scraped along the road, its horse bucking against the sudden drag and slowing. The driver shook his fist and yelled after them, but Crocus drove his horses on, separating them from the downed chariot.

John watched the man disappear into the distance, and only when he was sure they were long gone did he allow himself to breathe out. Or at least, that's how it felt. And with that breath, an exhaustion overwhelmed him.

The wagon slowed to a more reasonable pace, bumping over the stones in a rhythm that became almost predictable. John's eyelids grew heavy. Lying in the hay, he yawned, comfortable in his cozy little spot next to his big sister. He stared at the sky and clouds above. He couldn't hold his eyes open any longer.

The last thing John saw before he drifted off was Sarah, scowling at the deep dark valley at the end of the road.

CHAPTER TWELVE

A Close Encounter

SARAH

Sarah's stomach growled. She looked down at John, who had fallen asleep in the hay of the rocking cart. A yawn suddenly crept into her throat and she couldn't help but let it out. Must be all of the adrenaline they'd used up. The scare from the lion, Lucas's brawl with the soldiers, Roman legionaries who tried to arrest them, a chariot chase, and now, after all that action . . . trundling lazily along in a horse and cart toward what looked like Mount Doom from *The Lord of the Rings*. The dark foreboding clouds did not look inviting.

It was getting colder too. She snuggled Crocus's cloak closer to her body and hunched down next to her little brother. He had on a warm tunic—as well as his shorts and Nuggets shirt—and didn't seem bothered by the chill, though he was curled up into a tight ball.

Sarah heaped some sweet-smelling hay on top of him as a blanket. He squirmed.

"I'm hungry," she said to Crocus.

"Me too," he replied, as if this was a typical feeling, one he was used to.

"Here," Aurora said. She pulled a small white brick from her leather satchel and offered it. The little biscuit looked old and dry like a flattened stale dinner roll.

Sarah took it and brought it to her nose for a smell. It sort of smelled like salty bread.

Aurora giggled. "Never had hardtack before?"

"Hardtack?"

"I like to pretend it's a sausage," Crocus said with a grin.

"Oh!" Aurora lit up. "You have to try this thing called *Libum*. My dominus let me—"

"Your captor, you mean," Crocus interrupted.

Aurora continued. "The magistrate. It was his favorite. It's a cheesecake served with warm honey. It's really good. That's what I'd imagine this hardtack to be right now."

"I'd still take a sausage," Crocus replied. "A big fat juicy one fresh from the fire, spitting animal fat and spices like my dad used to make it."

Sarah took a nibble of the rock-hard biscuit.

"Hardtack, huh?"

"What's that?" John asked, rubbing his eyes.

"Enjoy your nap?" Sarah tried to crack the biscuit in half but had to smack it on the edge of the cart to break it in pieces. She offered some to John.

"I'm thirsty." John licked his lips.

Aurora handed back a leather canteen in the shape of a large kidney bean with some kind of animal hair still attached. John held it up for a second, rubbed the animal fur—Sarah imagined goat—then tipped it back steeply and drank from it.

"Easy," Crocus said. "That has to last all of us until we can refill."

The cart ambled along the Roman road. The wind picked up as the dark clouds seemed to descend nearer to them.

"We're gonna need some fire and a shelter soon." Crocus had his face turned to the sky.

Sarah munched on her hardtack. Once her saliva got working on it, it sort of tasted like bread. Sort of. Sarah decided she wasn't that hungry anymore, but thought it would be rude to throw it out or offer it back, so she tucked it into her pocket and took a conservative swig from the canteen.

"When can get back to the emperor?"

"Why would you want to go back?" Crocus asked.

"You—I—we need to talk with him."

Crocus muttered something under his breath.

Aurora spoke. "Maybe a raid when the Romans are fat after their holiday for Dies Natalis Solis Invicti." She looked to Crocus for agreement.

"Hard to say" was his reply. His face revealed little. "We need to find the others first."

"Well, you're full of helpful information." Sarah crossed her arms when he shot her a straight-faced glare. "When is Dies Natal-whatever?"

"You know the Romans could kill you. What's so important that you need to speak with that murderer?" Crocus didn't look back, his eyes on the road ahead.

"You need to unite with him!" John blurted.

Aurora giggled and shot Crocus a look.

"What do you think of that, little P?" Crocus asked Aurora.

"You know I don't like that name," she replied. "And I think it sounds like quite a plot."

Crocus laughed from the belly at that. "You do like a good plot."

"Soooo, when is that holiday?" Sarah asked again.

"Dies Natalis Solis Invicti is what the Romans call the birthday of their god Sol. The birthday of the Unconquered Sun," Aurora explained. She seemed immensely older than she looked.

"How old are you, anyway?" John asked.

"I'm nine."

"Nine? Wow. I'm ten, but—wow."

"Can someone please just answer my question?" Sarah shook her hands. "When is the sun's birthday?" The question sounded funny. "Soon, I hope?"

"December twenty-fifth, near the winter solstice, when the days start getting longer again," Crocus answered.

"You mean, like, the same day as Christmas?" John asked.

Aurora frowned and shook her head like she'd never heard of it.

"Okay, now we're getting somewhere," Sarah said, impatient. "What is today? How long until Christma— I mean, December twenty-fifth?"

"Saturnalia just began, so in a week or so, I think," Crocus said.

"Saturnalia—was that the party going on down there?" John waggled his head back and forth and stuck out his tongue, which made Aurora giggle.

"That's about it. They're supposed to be honoring their god Saturn, but it's basically a big excuse for everyone to do whatever they want. All the rules are ignored, slaves are allowed to walk free, people overeat and overdrink and gamble and—"

"Wait, you said that slaves are allowed to walk free?" Sarah asked, looking to Aurora. "Why weren't you allowed out, then?"

Crocus huffed. "No one would trust an Alemanni slave to return."

The cart bumped over a rock and interrupted the conversation as Crocus turned onto a side road, less well maintained. It was practically just an animal trail, and the wagon barely fit. The forest closed them in, the strong scent of spruce and fir and pine like vanilla and chocolate and butterscotch.

They ambled along until one side of their path cleared of trees like a curtain pulled back to reveal a spectacular view. Peaks of stiff, steep granite towered across from them like sentinels of the valley. John peered over the edge of the wagon and the frightening drop-off made him scoot up against the slope side of their carriage. The wind threw the tops of the trees back and forth. The sun had lowered enough that soon it would disappear behind a high mountain. The temperature dropped further.

"It's like *Lord of the Rings*," John mumbled, his teeth chattering.

"I was thinking the same thing. Maybe your pendant is the precious?" Sarah chided, batting his necklace with her hand.

John grasped the jade symbol and grunted at her.

"See? You're acting like Gollum already."

"Hilarious," John said.

Just then Sarah banged into the headboard when

Crocus suddenly yanked on the reins and the cart came to an abrupt halt.

Crocus jumped from the bench. "There's a patrol coming down the path."

Sarah looked far up the side of the mountain and saw a single-file group of horses carrying Roman legionaries, the familiar red and bronze armor clearly identifying them as dangerous. She looked back down the trail, but there was nowhere they could turn the cart around.

"We'll have to ditch the wagon and head up that slope by foot through those woods," Crocus said. "That should hide us, and we're not too far off, anyway. You three go now and I'll take care of this," he said as he unlatched the harness from the first horse.

John looked to Sarah for direction, and for a moment she resented him for it. Always looking to her to make his decisions for him. She jumped out of the wagon and followed Aurora into the forest, John close behind.

Sarah stopped and turned to watch Crocus push the cart at an angle to the path and then—oh no! He wheeled the cart to the edge of the cliff. It tottered for a second, then disappeared in an instant as if a trapdoor had opened underneath it. A few seconds later, she heard the impact far below.

Crocus grabbed two heavy wool blankets from the back of each horse, then slapped them on the rump, and they went tearing off down the path.

Just as Crocus reached the others in their hiding place behind a dense stand of trees, the Roman patrol passed by below. With the clouds and fading sunlight, the angle of the terrain, and their distance from the path, they didn't get a good look at the soldiers except for their shiny armor and a man at the front holding a large pole with a bronze eagle at the top. It reminded Sarah of the scepter she'd held in the museum, except this one was taller than a person and had a small red flag with gold tassels.

Lightning flashed, surprising a yelp from John. Sarah clapped her hand over his mouth, but the soldiers below did not turn their heads. The thunder boomed, echoing through the valley like cannon fire.

When the soldiers were out of sight, Sarah turned to see Crocus already trudging up the hill. He stopped and waved to them. "Up here. A perfect spot to rest for the night."

Sarah had done plenty of camping with her family and was happy to do more, but she'd never done so without a tent and a sleeping bag. She looked around at the "perfect" spot: a small clearing with matted-down dried grass. Crocus had started propping a few of the larger fallen branches to create a lean-to shelter. Sarah and John followed Aurora's lead and tore off some live branches full of needles, then added them to the roof.

It didn't actually look so bad. They had room for four to sleep, two big blankets, and each other. It was good enough. It would have to be.

John grabbed his stomach. "I'm hungry." His tone soured Sarah's optimism.

"Here," Sarah snapped, handing him the last of her hardtack. "Quit whining."

John snatched the biscuit, then lashed out and slugged her in the shoulder. "I'm not whining."

"Stop!" she shouted at him, rubbing her shoulder. She growled and bit her lip. Having a brother could be such a pain, literally.

John leapt away, anticipating a retaliatory attack, and escaped behind Crocus, who was assembling sticks into a tepee shape with one hand.

Sarah scowled and jabbed her finger toward John as if trying to shoot lightning from its tip. She could feel the steam starting up inside of her, but instead of going after her brother, she took off into the woods to cool down.

"Wait!" Crocus yelled after her. "Don't go alone."

But that's exactly what she wanted: to be alone.

CHAPTER THIRTEEN

Fenrir

JOHN

"She'll be back," John said to Crocus, who stood and rubbed his hand on his thigh.

"She really shouldn't go out there. It's getting dark."

Aurora stood up. "I'll go get her."

Crocus grabbed her arm. "Find her and come straight back here." His serious tone and stare gave John the willies.

"Don't worry." Aurora acted so confident that it made her seem much older than her real age. John looked at her and wondered where she was from, what had brought her here. Who *was* she?

Crocus held her arm a moment longer, then let go and scanned the forest. To John, he said, "Better get this fire going. Gather more wood and put it here."

John hopped to action. It was nice to have a job. And an easy job, at that.

"Sisters are tough, right?" John asked.

"I wouldn't know," Crocus answered.

"Aurora's not your sister?"

"No."

John waited for more detail, but none came. "Okay."

Crocus sighed and softened up. "But she might as well be. I've known her since she was a baby. I guess I protect her like she's my real sister."

John hung his head. Did he protect his sister, his real sister? He suddenly felt bad about slugging her in the arm. He was just tired. But that wasn't an excuse to treat her that way.

Crocus took a flint from somewhere within his tunic and struck it into the kindling. A few scratches later and a small fire smoldered. As if on cue, light snowflakes suddenly appeared, wafting all around like ash. After they had a nice little pile of wood to burn, John sat next to the fire, rubbing his hands in the growing flames.

Crocus looked into the shadows and said to himself, loud enough for John to overhear, "Come on, Aurora. You should be back by now."

A twig snapped in the forest. Crocus's body went taut. He looked around and picked up a suitable fist-size rock. Then he whistled his warbling birdsong. No reply.

John had been staring into the fire, and the night had grown dark quickly, so his eyes wouldn't focus into the inky blackness surrounding them. Snowflakes appeared in the aura of the flames and sizzled into nonexistence. His breath puffed out as a visible cloud and dissipated. He perked up his ears, listening, motionless.

Then John's breath caught in his throat. Two red eyes glowed at the edge of the tree line. "Th-there!" He pointed, but as soon as he did, the hovering fireballs disappeared.

Crocus spun in the direction John had pointed, but it was too late.

A second later, an ominous howl echoed through the canyon, a lament-filled ballad of loneliness.

"Wolves." Crocus put his hand to his mouth to channel his yell: "Aurora! Sarah!"

John swallowed. Another scuffle of branches in the dark made him yip with fear. Crocus heard that one too, the stone cocked back in his fist and ready to be hurled at the approaching wild creature. John imagined bared fangs lunging for them, claws like knives ripping at their clothes. Would Crocus's little rock make any difference? Who would the wolves attack first? Probably the scrumptious-looking smaller one, right?

The outline of a human appeared, and John exhaled in relief. Aurora entered the circumference of the firelight.

"Where's Sarah?" John asked.

"She's behind me. She wanted a few more minutes."

"No." John looked to Crocus. "We have to go get her." By *we*, he meant *you*.

Aurora cocked her head, asking for more detail.

"John thinks he may have seen a wolf," Crocus said. "You two stay here, near the fire. They won't bother you if you have fire."

John took a good-size log from the pile and chucked it into the blaze.

Aurora sat down next to John, her teeth chattering as she rubbed her hands in front of the flames. John unfurled one of the blankets and put it over her shoulders. She smiled in thanks.

A minute later, Sarah returned.

"Phew," John said.

She acted as if nothing had happened and gestured to the blanket around Aurora. "Oh, I want some of that."

John gave her the second blanket and she responded with a subtle "Thanks."

"Welcome," John said. He wanted to apologize for hitting her earlier, but it seemed harder than just not acknowledging it at all. Maybe giving her the blanket said enough.

He poked at the red-hot coals with a stick, sending embers like fiery faeries dancing into the night.

"So, where's Crocus?" Sarah asked. She shook her head toward the fire, sending a few snowflakes to their doom.

"I'm here," he said, emerging as a ghost might, suddenly, with a thin coat of snow on his shoulders. "And there you are. I was looking for you."

"I'm here." Sarah smiled.

Crocus smiled back. "Glad you're safe."

Did Sarah's cheeks just flush?

"And Aurora. Glad you're both safe, I mean. John too. Glad we're all safe." Crocus was definitely acting strange all of a sudden.

The fire popped and John jumped.

Crocus cocked an eye and cast a sly grin. "I think we need a good campfire story." He couldn't have timed it better: a wolf across the valley howled its lonely song. "And I know just the one."

"Is it scary?" John asked.

"It is a tale of sacrifice and mercy, and honor among gods," Crocus said. Then, putting his chin nearer the flames to cast eerie shadows over his face, he said, "And yes, it's very scary."

John squirmed a little. "Oh—okay, fine, cool. I love

scary stories. Totally fine."

Sarah rolled her eyes at Crocus, but the corner of her mouth was turned up in a subtle smile.

"What? No, it'll be fine," John said. "Let's hear it."

"The story of Fenrir the wolf." Crocus snarled and bit the air, his fingers curled like claws.

John jumped at another perfectly timed howl. "You've gotta be kidding me."

All three of them, except John, laughed at that.

"I'm still hungry," John said. Scary movies always made him want to munch on something too.

Aurora pulled a biscuit out of her bag. "This is the last one." She looked to Crocus.

"I'll go hunting tomorrow," Crocus said, gesturing to Aurora to give the last hardtack to John.

John hesitated taking it, as if he was taking food away from a homeless person who needed it more. That's what they were, right? He remembered back to the hearty pancake breakfast he'd eaten that morning. What had a slave and a venator eaten for breakfast?

Aurora sensed his hesitation and thrust the biscuit toward him, insisting.

John's stomach whined. "Thank you," he said softly, taking the food.

Crocus continued, "I think it's only a day or two more before we reach the camp. But we'll be on foot. Will you two be okay with that?"

"We can hike," Sarah said, confident. "But I do wish I had some warmer clothes." She tugged the thick wool blanket around her head. John shivered, envious of Sarah warm in her covering. The fire warmed the front of John's body and face, but his back was to the cold night air. At least he was protected from the falling snow by the lean-to under which he sat with Aurora. Sarah and Crocus sat exposed, but Crocus didn't even shiver. John rotated around to warm his backside.

"Here," Aurora said, holding open her blanket.

"You sure?"

Aurora laughed. "Of course."

John caught Sarah glancing toward Crocus. She opened her blanket and looked like she was about to offer him some blanket just like Aurora had offered John, then she rearranged her grip and cinched it tighter to herself. Crocus didn't seem to notice the missed opportunity.

As John huddled closer to the girl, Crocus began his tale. "Fenrir was a giant wolf the size of an elephant, a child of Loki, that mischievous rascal." He tapped Aurora on the nose, and she giggled. Okay, maybe she really was only nine.

"At his birth, the gods prophesied that Fenrir would someday destroy all the cosmos." Crocus waved his hand to encompass the full width of the night sky. Looking up, John noticed the stars had come out, which made him realize the snow had stopped too. Just a dusting had fallen. John felt cozier under the blanket with Aurora's body heat warming him, the four of them sitting around the crackling campfire about to hear an ancient story of the gods. For a second, he actually felt calm and comfortable and—happy? Maybe if there were s'mores.

"The gods raised Fenrir in their palace at Asgard to keep a careful eye on him."

"So he wouldn't destroy the cosmos," Sarah snickered.

"Yes," Crocus said, shooting her a glance. "During this time, only Týr, upholder of law and honor, dared approach the beast to feed him. As Fenrir grew larger and fiercer, the gods decided they had to defend the cosmos and act by containing Fenrir."

"*Contain* him?" Sarah smirked. "They're gods. Can't they just snap their fingers or something?"

John thought about Aten. *The gods have chosen you*, he'd said.

Crocus paused and let his characteristic half grin settle on Sarah for a moment.

"Shhh," John said, nibbling on his hardtack, already engrossed in the story. "What next?"

"The gods told Fenrir they wanted to witness his great strength through a series of challenges. As vain as he was, Fenrir consented. Their first attempt to bind

Fenrir failed. With his massive jaws, Fenrir bit easily through the chain." Crocus snapped his jaws shut and growled. "The gods cheered and clapped to keep up the ruse, then tried another chain, twice as strong, but Fenrir sliced through it with his enormous claws as if he were gutting a fish. The gods' concern only grew with each failed attempt. Odin, the mighty god of wisdom and war, father of Týr, sent for help from the dark dwarves in the underground mines. The same dwarves who made Thor's hammer. With their skill at crafting, the dwarves made a set of shackles from the sound of a cat's feet, the beard of a woman, the root of a mountain, the breath of a fish, and the spit of a bird."

John wrinkled his nose.

"These are things which do not exist and are therefore impossible to struggle against. Gleipnir was its name. But when the gods challenged Fenrir to another show of his immense strength, the wolf was suspicious of the new chains forged by the dwarves. He would not allow them to bind him until he had a show of good faith. And that is when brave Týr, for the good of all the cosmos, volunteered his hand to rest in the open jaws of the wolf on behalf of all the gods."

Crocus put his left hand to his open mouth and snarled. Sarah grimaced playfully, going along with the drama.

"Fenrir accepted the pledge and allowed himself to

be bound by Gleipnir. But the wolf quickly realized he had been tricked; he could not escape from Gleipnir, and angered by the betrayal, he bit off Týr's hand—" Crocus chomped his jaws together in an audible click and ripped at his own hand. Then, in a flash, he dropped his left arm behind his back and raised the stump of his right. He paused, teeth bared, his stump clear in the firelight.

John's eyes were wide, and he could practically see the sinews between the wolf's teeth and Týr's arm spurting blood.

"The other gods cheered for Fenrir's execution, but Týr demanded mercy. Even so, he realized they could not just let the wolf loose, so they looped the chain of Gleipnir through a giant stone slab anchored with an even larger block. A sword was forced into his jaws to keep them open. He howled wildly and never ending, but Fenrir was *contained*." He winked at Sarah. She giggled but suppressed her reaction as quickly as she'd given in to it.

"That's it?" John asked. "What happened to Fenrir?"

"The rest of Fenrir's story is for another campfire and tells the tale of Ragnarök, the doom of the gods."

"And Týr?"

"Týr saved our world, and he did it with mercy. He watches over us now." Crocus rubbed his hand over his stump. "He and I share a bond. We both fight for justice and our people, and we're willing to sacrifice, if we must." With that, he looked down and stirred the fire.

John stared at him, images of gods and dark dwarves and the demonic Fenrir with eyes glowing red like the wolf he'd seen earlier.

"We should get some sleep," Aurora said.

Yeah, right, John thought.

CHAPTER FOURTEEN

A Realization Dawns

SARAH

Sarah lay on the forest floor under the blanket, staring wide-eyed at the stars through the ring of tree crowns framing her view. The coals from the fire glowed nearby. She'd been camping with her family many times, and she'd seen starscapes before, but never like this. She felt closer to the cosmos and—she reached out her hand, her fingers swirling in the cosmic stew—it was almost like she could touch them.

But, really, she just wanted to sleep. Dog-tired and who knew what was in store for them tomorrow, she *needed* to sleep. The more she thought about it, the harder it became. Her eyes burned and she ached to pass out, but her mind wouldn't let her.

Thoughts nagged at her. Why hadn't the eye of Ra worked? What were they doing out here? Did they really have a "quest" like Aten had said? Would that help them get home? Why had this happened to her—to them—again? They were "chosen"? Sarah didn't believe in gods, but she hadn't believed in time travel either. What other options were there? They'd seen Constantius. And now they were with Crocus. But how could she get those two together? They clearly weren't on the best of terms.

She remembered back to their trip to ancient Egypt. She'd traced the eye of Ra in the cave, the flash of light, adventures, new friends, Imhotep, tomb robber, et cetera et cetera, then they'd found the right carving in the pyramid, the same one that had brought them back in time, and she'd traced that one again and they returned home. Easy-peasy, right? What was she missing?

John had traced the eye of Ra pendant in the museum to bring them here. But when he'd traced the eye here to take them back—wait. Wait!

Sarah sat up, pulling the blanket accidentally off John a little. He squirmed and pulled it back up.

She had traced the eye of Ra here several times, but had John? The first time they time hopped, Sarah had traced the symbol to get them there *and* to get them back. This time, John had transported them, so—

"Of course!"

She turned to John and shook his shoulder, whispering, "John, wake up."

"Huh?" John blinked his eyes.

"Wake up."

"Wrong?" He usually spoke in single words when half-asleep.

"I think I know how to get home."

That got his eyes to open. He sat up but didn't say anything.

Sarah thought about the flash, eager to feel it carry them through time. But she glanced at Crocus and Aurora, asleep, remembering when the flash in Egypt had dragged along their ancient friends, as it had Lucas. But not Aten, she realized. Hm. Maybe because he had been unconscious? So maybe it wouldn't take the people sleeping either? No reason to test that theory.

"Be quiet, but follow me."

"What?"

"Just do it," she snipped.

John stood and wrapped the blanket around his shoulders and followed Sarah into the woods. "Wolves."

"That won't be a problem as soon as we get a little ways away from Crocus and Aurora," Sarah said, moving him along faster than his feet were carrying him. *As soon as we get away from Crocus and Aurora.* That made her stop in her tracks and look back to their two new friends. That's what they were now—friends, right? Could she just leave without saying goodbye?

She found a wall of a boulder blocking them from the campsite and went behind it.

Sarah put her hands on John's shoulders and smiled. "It's you."

"Me?"

"You have to trace the eye of Ra to get us home. You traced it to get us here. So you have to get us back."

"I— Didn't I already?"

Sarah shook her head, smiling, giddy with hope. Her arm hairs tingled. "I don't think you have. Or I hope you haven't, because then my idea is— I think we should try it."

"Shouldn't we tell Crocus and Aurora?" John asked.

"I know," Sarah said. "I feel bad too. But what would we tell them? 'We're gonna travel back to the future now, see ya round.' We'll miss them, but if this is a real chance to get home, then I think we have to try it. Don't you?"

"Okay." He looked back to their sleeping friends.

"Think of Mom and Dad, Johnny."

"Yeah." John pulled the pendant out of his shirt. "Hey, maybe if this works, we can come back to tell Crocus about uniting with Constantius. Maybe we can still complete the mission."

Sarah was starting to lose patience. "Sure, John, just do it."

John started tracing the almond eye. Then he stopped to rub sleep out of his own eye and yawned.

"What are you doing? Just trace it!" She shook him.

"Okay, okay." John moved his finger around the eye, the brow, the line with the curlicue finish. As his finger finished down the line with the knifelike edge, Sarah held her breath and closed her eyes. This was it!

A moment passed. Then another. No strobe of bright light. No flash.

She opened one eye. John was tracing the eye of Ra again.

"No," Sarah said. "No." She took the pendant from John and traced it with her own finger. Twice. Nothing.

She clenched her jaw and held her breath, felt the vein in her neck bulge. Sarah desperately wanted to let out an ear-shattering scream of frustration—she had to let it vent or it would pop a neuron—but she knew she had to contain it.

Contain it. Ha, like Fenrir. Thinking of Crocus's grin, his pale blue eyes reflecting the firelight, she breathed and looked at John, who was cringing as if a nuclear bomb might go off any minute.

"Didn't work," John said.

Sarah laughed at that obvious and simple comment.

In a flash, her emotions eased back from rocket-launch mode. "It didn't work," she repeated. She looked over to Crocus and Aurora. Maybe it was okay that it hadn't worked. Maybe they really did need to finish this "quest" before they could go back home. A little more time with Crocus wouldn't be terrible. Her head felt heavy and light at the same time. Exhaustion finally came flooding in.

"We'll figure it out. We always do, right?" John said. "Can we go back to sleep now?"

"Sleep. Yes." Sarah dragged herself back to camp.

Crocus sat up. "Everything okay?"

"No," Sarah said, plopping down under the shelter. "Or maybe. I don't know." She laid on her back and stared out through the hole in the treetops at the universe expanding before her.

"We're . . . just tired," John said. He lay down next to her and arranged the blanket over them.

"So tired," Sarah said, yawning.

Crocus didn't move, his eyes—that pale blue icy stare—scanning the darkness for a few moments longer. Then he lay down too.

Sarah noticed that Crocus had a good-size rock tight in his fist. She didn't need him, no, but it felt good to know he was protecting them.

CHAPTER FIFTEEN

The Scar-Faced Roman

JOHN

John often woke up before his older sister no matter if they were at home on a school day or they were out camping. John was the early riser.

His internal clock flipped his eyes open well before the sun had unrolled its first rays over the edge of the monumental Alps, but the dim predawn light was enough to spur John into a new day. He wasn't in any hurry to get up, though. Crocus and Aurora still snoozed, and it was freezing cold outside of the blanket. The fire had died to almost nothing. John grabbed a few more twigs nearby, including the poker stick he'd been using last night, tossed them onto the coals, then blew into the embers to flare them back to life. The twigs caught, and the tiny fire grew for warming duty. It encouraged John to add more wood, so he carefully slid out of the blanket, careful not to disturb his sister.

The movement roused Crocus, and he startled, sitting up in a burst, holding a rock in his hand.

"Morning," John said, then yawned.

Crocus scratched his head. "Morning." Then he ambled off into the trees, presumably for a morning bathroom visit.

Sarah stirred and grunted.

"Good morning!" Aurora grinned. She bounced up out of her sleeping spot and had the blanket rolled almost instantly.

John beamed a smile at her enthusiasm. Another morning person!

With a few more sticks, including some pine cones, John built the fire back up to a steady blaze. Crocus returned with a long straight branch the circumference of a broom handle.

"That looks too green to burn," John commented. He'd burned many a branch while camping, experimenting with anything he could get his hands on, within reasonable safety standards, of course.

Crocus crouched next to a slab of stone. "This isn't for burning." He started rubbing the wood at an angle along the rock.

The first ray of sun broadcast itself over the ridge and John soaked it up, closing his eyes and letting it hit him full force. "Feels warmer already." A bird trilled. John took a deep breath of the crisp mountain air. "I—I have a feeling it's going to be a good day."

Aurora smiled and nodded at him. "And so it shall be."

Sarah growled. "Ugh." She rolled over and pulled the blanket over her head.

"What're you making?" John asked Crocus.

He stopped scraping and held up the end of the stick, now shaped into a dull point. "Almost there."

"A spear. Cool."

"For hunting," Crocus said, turning back to his task. "Or protection." Still scraping, he peered back at John for a reaction.

"From the wolves?" John asked.

"There are more dangerous things than wolves."

"You mean the Romans."

"Or whomever the enemy may be."

Aurora interrupted. "No reason to sit around here. Let's get going."

A few more strokes of the spear on the stone, and Crocus seemed satisfied, testing its sharp point with his finger while holding it in the crook of his right elbow against his body.

"Aye. Let's go," he said. This was aimed primarily at

Sarah, still lying down.

Sarah rolled over to face the fire with a vacant stare.

"Come on, up and at 'em," John said, clapping.

Sarah scowled at him, but it was mostly a tease. She stood and stretched, reaching her hands toward the sky.

With the fire smothered, they headed up the narrow trail. They hiked in breathtakingly beautiful country. Around every bend, John kept thinking, *This looks like a postcard.*

The trail widened and Crocus stopped, then held up his left hand in a *stop* gesture.

"What?" Aurora whispered.

Crocus didn't respond. He cocked his ear.

Then they all heard it. Horses, the clink of armor.

Could it be the Alemanni raiders they were trying to find?

John felt a glimmer of hope. "Knew it would be a good day," he said to Sarah.

"Shh." Crocus put his finger to his lips.

"Isn't that your clan or tribe or whatever?" John asked.

"Hide," Crocus responded, darting off the trail and into the woods.

Sarah grabbed John's arm and they ran, then crouched behind the boulder with Crocus and Aurora.

John didn't need to ask any more questions. They'd

hidden without a moment to lose. Around a bend in the mountain slope, down the trail came a group of armed Roman legionaries mounted on horses. Eight men in all, single file. The leader had a deep purple scar running diagonally across his face, over the bridge of his nose. The man behind him held a golden staff with an eagle statuette and a red flag with gold tassels. He wore a real lion's head atop his helmet. The effect was menacing. These were not random guards from the magistrate; these looked like more experienced warriors.

The horses had on something like iron shoes, not just horseshoes—the coverings partially encased their hooves like an actual sandal. The men had glimmering bronze armor that clanked as their horses jaunted down the trail. They sounded like a war machine.

Crocus gasped, then gripped his spear and gritted his teeth. "That's him."

"Who?" John whispered.

"The man that killed my father. That centurion with the scar." He cocked back his arm to hurl the makeshift spear.

Aurora put her hand on his arm to block the throw. "Not now."

"Move!" Crocus swatted her hand aside, eliciting a surprised look of fear on Aurora's face that made him pause. His eyes darted to the scar-faced Roman, then back to Aurora, then back to the man who had killed his father.

"Not now," Aurora said, placing her hand on his chest.

The spear shook in his hand, but he lowered his aim. "We *are* outnumbered."

"We'll get the others and find him when we have the advantage," Aurora said.

Crocus gritted his teeth and shook his head. "I hate it when you're right."

"Shh." Aurora pointed toward the trail.

The horses had stopped. The scar-faced leader held up a hand, commanding his men to be quiet. They listened.

John couldn't move. An icy sweat sprang from his hair follicles. The lump in his throat wouldn't let him swallow. The sound of his own heart beating in his ears was so loud he was sure that the soldiers would hear it and come charging after them.

Terrifying seconds passed.

"Do you think it was the escaped slaves, Marcus?" the man wearing the lion's head asked the scar-faced Roman.

"I don't know."

"Don't know why those two should be worth so much trouble."

"It's important to our emperor to capture them

alive," Marcus replied.

"Do you mean Constantius or Allectus?" the lion-headed man asked.

"Quiet, you fool!" Marcus snapped. "The woods may have ears, and we wouldn't want our plan to be exposed too early, now, would we?" Marcus smacked the man on the back of the head.

"Sorry, centurion." The man bowed in shame while nervously darting his glance back and forth, as if someone had overheard him.

Then Marcus barked an order, and John nearly yipped at the suddenness of it.

The legionaries restarted their patrol behind their officer, kicking their heels into the horses to get them moving.

John glanced at Crocus, whose face was contorted in a twist of rage and sorrow, as if angry tears might spring from his bloodshot eyes.

After several minutes, until they couldn't hear the clank and clamor of the Romans' descent on the mountain trail any longer, without a word Crocus stomped off up the trail.

CHAPTER SIXTEEN

A Little Mercy

SARAH

When the Romans stopped, Sarah thought she heard something too. The soldiers could have stopped because they heard Crocus talking, but Sarah had also picked up the whine of some animal. Was it a dog? No, it sounded like a puppy, whimpering. Strangely, as soon as the clatter of the horses and armor ceased, so did the plaintive cry from the pup. But it sounded close. Maybe up the hill a little. The origin of a sound can be deceiving in the mountains, but Sarah scanned the hillside above them.

As soon as the soldiers had gone, Crocus stormed to the trail, but Sarah started up the steep embankment, loose rock tumbling from her footsteps.

"What're you doing?" John asked. He was always asking that.

"Sounds like a puppy needs help."

She didn't look back to see if they were following her.

A thunderous howl jolted her reflexively low to the ground, as if the sky itself were falling.

Wait. Of course it wouldn't be a dog out here in the woods, but it could be a—

The ominous howl again, probably echoing for miles by its strength.

Curiosity got the better of her, and she peeked around a boulder and saw an enormous black-furred wolf guarding the entrance to a small cave, or more like a small hole. If it was their burrow, she had no idea how that huge creature could fit in there.

Yip!

There, *that* was the whimpering she'd heard before, and it hadn't come from the big bad wolf; it had come from within the little hole.

Then she saw it. A tiny wolf pup stuck its furry nose out of the rocky earth and gave the cutest little puppy howl, crying to its mom. Sarah's heart ached, and she let out an audible "Awwwww."

The huge wolf snapped its jaws toward Sarah's hiding place behind the boulder. It had a patch of white fur between its fierce eyes staring directly at her.

Sarah froze. A low rumbling growl shook the wolf's upper lip.

"Back away!" Crocus yelled, suddenly appearing on the other side of the clearing with his spear held in front of him. He gestured to Sarah to go.

John suddenly showed up too, tugging at Sarah's dress. "Come on!"

Sarah hesitated, then the wolf pup yipped again, and her heart cracked into a million pieces. She stepped out from behind the boulder.

"Wait!" she yelled to Crocus, waving her arms above her head.

The wolf spread its front paws and lowered its head, ready to pounce.

"What. Are. You. Doing?!" John was a frantic mess.

"Hold on," Sarah said, gesturing with her shaking palms to both Crocus and John. When she looked over at her brother, she saw Aurora there too. Aurora was focused on the wolf, but her calm seemed surprising, given the primal animal growling at Sarah.

"I think the pup is trapped," Sarah said.

"So what?!" John had clumps of his hair in his hands. "Get back here!"

Sarah approached the huge wolf with slow cautious steps, her eyes locked on its eyes, that patch of white fur in between. Her arms were out in a universal symbol of *I'm not going to hurt you.*

"This is not Fenrir," Crocus said. "You're not saving the cosmos."

"He's big enough to be," Aurora added.

Sarah advanced. The wolf made a false attack, lunging forward a step, then backing up, its enormous paws skittering in the dirt. Sarah froze but did not retreat.

"Sh, sh, sh, it's okay," she told the creature. "I'm gonna help you and free your pup there." She pointed.

The wolf growled and snapped its jaws at the air. Sarah winced but held her ground.

One more step and she could practically pet the wolf, whose head came level to her own, the fierce unblinking eyes boring though her. She swallowed the lump in her throat and took another step. "It's okay."

The world faded around her as a blur. All of her attention was on portraying to the wolf that she meant no harm. Her movements were slow and measured like she imagined a Zen monk's might be.

"Look," she heard Aurora whisper.

The wolf moved aside from the hole. The pup noticed the shadow of her massive bulk disappear and it yipped in fear.

Sarah knelt down closer to where the pup was trapped. Then, it took every ounce of her strength, but she looked away from the giant wolf. She could imagine its hot breath on her neck.

The tiny pup's wet nose poked out of the hole, its tiny tongue whipping about. Despite being watched over by a carnivorous beast, Sarah couldn't help grinning at the little pup.

With great effort, she pulled and heaved and eventually rolled the stone trapping the pup in its prison. The pup whimpered and cowered toward the back of the dark hole, but Sarah reached in, grabbed it by the scruff of the neck, and pulled it to her chest in a hug. The pup's snuggly fur against her cheek and its tiny tongue on her chin like rough sandpaper made Sarah giggle.

When she turned to face her friends, terror gripped her. The giant wolf was in mid-air leaping toward her. She hadn't even heard it jump. Its great body slammed into hers and knocked her and the pup to the ground.

Sarah put her arms up to guard her face, her eyes closed. The wet-dog stench was so strong she could taste it; its acrid breath burned her nostrils. She wanted to yell out for Mom, for Dad, even to John—but she couldn't. Her breath was caught and her heart had stopped.

And then she realized the wolf hadn't torn her to pieces. Yet. She was still alive. *Right?*

As evidence, her heart beat heavy and loud in her ears.

She opened her eyes to see the giant wolf's snout

right in front of her face, its tongue lolling inches from her nose. Then it pressed closer and Sarah shut her eyes again.

But instead of taking a bite, the wolf licked her with its rough slobbery tongue on one cheek, then when Sarah flopped her head, it licked the other. Then it slathered her forehead and chin and even her hair. It kept licking and licking until Sarah couldn't help but let out the best gut laugh she'd had since—since—well, probably since they moved from Colorado to Maryland. The pup joined in too, adding its scratchy little tickly tongue and cold nose to the mix.

Sarah, laughing loud, reached out and suddenly both the wolf and its pup were gone in a flash, leaping up the mountainside as smoothly as a stream. Sarah couldn't stop her nervous, giddy laughing as they disappeared in the blink of an eye.

Crocus closed the distance across the clearing and skidded to his knees next to Sarah. "Are you okay? Where are you hurt?" He put his hand on her face and smoothed back her rumpled red hair, touched her forehead, her neck, searching for wounds.

Sarah just giggled more. "You're tickling me!"

"I—I can't believe it," Crocus said.

"I'm fine," Sarah said. His pale blue eyes conveyed such concern staring into hers. It made her relax and smile. "Thank you."

"I'm glad you're not hurt," he said. He sounded genuinely relieved and Sarah felt warm and embarrassed at his concern.

John interrupted. "Do you have a death wish?!" He shook his hands in the air.

Crocus laughed. He leaned aside and lay down next to her, staring at the sky, muttering something to Týr.

Aurora smiled in a wise and loving way. "Even a lone wolf needs help once in a while."

CHAPTER SEVENTEEN

Invaders

JOHN

After they'd recovered from the wolf incident—well, actually, John wasn't sure he'd ever recover from the sight of the wolf lunging at his sister. He'd screamed and watched, rooted in his spot. He wanted to close his eyes, but he couldn't look away. The shock dissipated slightly when he saw his sister laughing, replaced by a deep love and relief.

John reached for his sister's hand swinging in front of him as they walked up the steep mountain trail. They'd been hiking for several hours after the wolf incident, mostly not talking. John's thoughts kept flashing back to the sight of the wolf flying like an avalanche of black stone, falling on top of Sarah. His throat tightened, and he just wanted to hold his sister's hand for a minute. Maybe it sounded silly, but he wanted her to know that—

She let him grab her hand for a step and a half, then realized it was there and shook it away. Not in a mean way, more like she was waving away a fly.

And that's exactly how John felt sometimes with her. Small. Brushed away. All he wanted was to take it all back. He wished he'd never traced the eye of Ra and brought them here. The pendant swayed on his neck in rhythm with his steps. For a moment, he wanted to rip it off and chuck it down the slope.

Sweat dripped off his forehead despite the chill in the air. The hike was steep, but fortunately their parents had trained them well with long climbs in the Rockies.

Still, John stopped a minute and leaned against a tree. He looked out over the glacial-carved valley far below. Two eagles with their wings outstretched soared on a thermal updraft, weaving around each other in a figure eight.

John inhaled a big lungful of the crisp Alps air. "Dad would like it here."

"So would Mom," Sarah added, startling John. He hadn't realized she'd stopped too.

"I know, yeah," John said, shifting his weight away from the tree to face her.

"Thirsty?" Sarah asked.

"You have water?" He realized his voice was raspy.

"No." Sarah looked up the trail at Crocus and Aurora, nearing the crest of a ridge line. "But I'm thirsty too. You doing okay?"

John stretched his back. "I'm good. You?"

"Yeah." He'd expected some kind of complaint, but she seemed like she authentically meant it. "Come on." Sarah clapped him on the back, then turned and restarted the hike.

John grinned and trudged after her.

A few minutes more of steep ascent and they crested the ridge. Over the hump, a gorgeous alpine lake sat serene in the sunlight, a crescent moon of ice layered around its edge. Mist wafted off it like hot soup. A spit of land projected into the center like a spoon resting in the middle of the bowl. The craggy mountains ringing the cirque reminded John of chunks of crusty sourdough bread. He suddenly tasted warm melted butter.

"I think I'm hungry."

Sarah licked her lips. "Me too."

Crocus and Aurora had descended and were at the lake's edge, cupping the water into their mouths.

John and Sarah looked at each other, then John smiled through cracked, dry lips and took off after his sister down to the water's edge. The crystal-clear lake was pure snow melt and the tastiest, coldest refreshment he'd ever tasted in all his life.

John took frequent mental snapshots, since this kind of alpine lake was his ideal mountain scene. He kept wishing he had his real camera so he could share the vision with his parents, though photos never captured the essence of the real thing.

When John looked across the lake, he saw movement high up the rock wall.

"Hey," he whispered. Crocus splashed water on his face. "Quiet, look."

Another flash of movement. John burped from the quantity of water he'd consumed. His belly sloshed.

"Baaaa!" Aurora cried out. It echoed. The animals didn't respond, but one turned its head toward them and stared.

"Quiet, little P." Crocus didn't even glance. "Don't know who else might be listening." He walked down the shoreline, examining the ground like he was looking for something.

John laughed. "Goats! Mountain goats, Sarah, look!"

Sure enough, six of the nimble creatures, including a baby kid, bounced around the narrow ledges of the cliff face with what seemed to be zero fear of their precarious hold on the mountainside.

"Wow," John said. "How do they stick to the rock like that?"

"Very carefully," Sarah joked.

"Actually, it's easy for them," Aurora chimed in.

Sarah laughed. "I know, I'm joking. We've seen mountain goats a few times in Colorado."

"I haven't heard of that land. Is that where you're from?"

Sarah cast her eyes down. "Well, it used to be. But now we live in Maryland."

"Strange. Never heard of that one either. Your home must be far from here."

"You could definitely say that," John added.

"You don't like it in Mare-eh-land?" Aurora asked. Sarah still had her head down.

"Oh, no, it's fine," Sarah answered. "I just didn't think I'd miss my friends so much. But it's fine."

John knew she was talking about Cynthia and Maxine. Sarah and those two had been pretty inseparable. Maybe that's why she'd been so moody lately.

"I miss Roman too," he said.

"I thought you might be Roman," Aurora said, "because you wear the *bulla*." She pointed to his pendant.

"Oh, no, Roman is my friend. I mean, my friend's name *is* Roman. Wait, he doesn't have a Roman name, his actual name is— Sarah, help me out here."

Sarah just giggled.

Aurora looked at John, puzzled, then pointed to his pendant. "I've never seen a bulla quite like that."

John held up his necklace. "This is the eye of Ra, I got it from an Egyptian . . ." He looked at Sarah.

"From a friend," she finished. "But not Roman." John laughed.

Sarah continued, "Aurora, if you thought we were Roman, why'd you help us? Crocus—" She lowered her voice and cast her eyes over at Crocus walking away down the shore. "Crocus *hates* the Romans."

Aurora turned to watch Crocus too. "He doesn't necessarily hate Romans. Well, except Marcus."

"Right."

"Crocus helped you because he is a good person and you were in trouble." Aurora said it as if it were simple.

Sarah smiled.

"We're not Roman," John reiterated.

"Okay. I just thought your bulla—" Aurora pointed again at John's pendant.

John shook his head. "What is a bulla?"

"Roman boys are given an amulet—called a bulla—to wear until they reach manhood. It's usually a locket, but given the shape of yours—the eye—I just assumed it was a bulla, since they're for protection from the evil eye. Girls get a crescent moon called a *lunula* to protect them, and I didn't see one on Sarah, so I assumed it was because she was married."

"Married?" Sarah spat, incredulous, though she blushed at the same time. "Why is everyone always trying to marry me off when we go back in time?"

Aurora squinted. "What d'you mean—'back in time'?"

"Oh, nothing. I just mean someone in Egypt tried to engage me to be married too."

"But you're not ready?" Aurora asked.

"I'm twelve!" Sarah exclaimed.

John laughed, but he wanted to change the subject back to something Aurora had said. "What's the evil eye?"

Aurora shrugged. "I don't believe in it. A curse caused by a malevolent glare? Only the gods have that power."

"You mean like—the stink eye?" Sarah chuckled and raised one eyebrow in a scowl at John.

John kept his attention on this girl only a year younger than him, but so mature it was weird. *Malevolent?* John had read that word in books before, and he knew it had to do with someone wishing bad on someone else, but who actually used that word in regular speech?

"Yeah, it's strange," Aurora said, apparently interpreting John's scrunched-up nose as agreement that curses couldn't be caused by the stink eye.

Crocus was heading back their way with a frown.

"What's wrong?" Aurora asked.

"They're gone."

"Who?" John asked.

"This was the secret meeting place for our Alemanni brothers raiding on this side of the Rhine," Crocus said. "But the camp has been abandoned."

Just then the mountain goats erupted into raucous bleating, echoing around the bowl of the lake. Dashing up the rock face as adept as if it were flat ground, they were escaping from something. John squinted and saw in the distance a group of people shooting arrows toward the goats. They weren't Romans.

"Are those your Alemanni tribe?" John asked, but when he looked at Aurora, he could tell from her wide eyes that they were not.

"Time to go," Crocus said, pushing them all into the forest.

"Those are *Helvetii*," Aurora answered.

"They're not friendly?" Sarah asked.

"I don't want to find out," Crocus said. "Ever since the Romans invaded their land here, their numbers have dwindled, and you could say they're pretty angry about anyone in their territory."

One of the goats scurrying up a cliff took an arrow and lost its footing. It went tumbling down the rocks. Sarah gasped and put her hand to her mouth.

"Since we're Alemanni," Aurora added, "they see us as invaders too."

The goat came to rest at the base of the slope, crying out. It was a heartrending sound.

"Yeah, let's get out of here," John said.

The goat eventually stopped its cry, and John knew that the Helvetii would be dining on goat meat tonight. Despite the thought of the poor creature's demise, John's stomach rumbled at the thought of fresh meat for dinner.

CHAPTER EIGHTEEN

A Rock and a Hard Place

SARAH

Sarah kept thinking, *How do we get home?*

She'd pondered that question a lot while hiking in silence up this huge mountain, but now that Crocus had said their rendezvous camp was abandoned, it was again the first question that sparked in her mind. Why were they following this handsome boy-warrior and this oddly wise little girl?

You must unite Constantius and Crocus, she reminded herself of Aten's words. But . . . *why?*

Something told her she wouldn't find the answer here in this time. Maybe back in her own time. Maybe Aten had those answers. The thought of meeting him again sent a shiver up her spine.

She missed her parents and her skateboard and her fully stocked refrigerator. So again she asked herself, *How do we get home?*

After the cave that transported them last time was crushed in a rockslide, the fragility of time traveling became plain to her. While gallivanting around ancient Egypt, she hadn't worried about being trapped there forever. But now she couldn't get it out of her mind. Would they be trapped here if they didn't fulfill the quest Aten had said was sent from the gods? It sounded unbelievable. But so did time travel, so—

Argh. Maybe she didn't have a choice but to accomplish this goal Aten set for them. Is that what it came down to? Sarah tightened her fists. The anger inside bubbled, the steam pushing at her chest. The lack of control over her own life made it feel as if the ground under her feet wasn't as stable as before. Before what? Before the move? Before . . . all of this. It wasn't fair. She wanted to go back to being how she was before, trotting around middle school with Cynthia and Maxine.

She knew she couldn't go back, and she didn't know who to be mad at about that. So, mostly, she blamed herself, just like John had blamed her. If she hadn't gone spelunking in that cave while John pleaded with her not to, if she hadn't traced that hieroglyph on the cave wall, none of this would have happened and they wouldn't even be here right now and—

"What do you think, Sarah?" John asked, as if it weren't the first time. They had all moved away from the lake, safely out of sight from the Helvetii on the other side.

"About what?" she snapped at him, and he pulled back, surprised by her sudden outburst.

"I found a potential trail," Crocus said. "I think we could track them."

"Who?" Sarah asked, her head still not quite in the present.

Crocus squinted at her. "Our Alemanni group. But we have no idea where they are, how far they've gone, or if they're still even in Roman territory. I have to get you home"—he nodded to Aurora—"so you're safe. But I've seen the scar-faced Roman—Marcus—and I need to avenge my father."

"So we go along with you on your revenge plot?" Sarah looked at John, then quickly back to Crocus. Every time she looked at her brother, guilt reared its ugly head. He reminded her that this was all her fault.

"That's up to you," Crocus said. In the way he said it, Sarah thought she heard hope that she'd agree to go with him.

"Why don't we flee north?" Aurora pitched in. "Sneak past the Roman defenses, cross the Rhine, and get to safety among our people in Alemannia."

Crocus massaged the scarred skin on his stump. He bit his lip and blinked his eyes as if making a terrible decision. "I can't. I can't leave now and miss my opportunity at the scar-faced Roman. I have to try. I'm sorry." He bowed his head.

"Don't be sorry," Aurora said.

"And we need you to partner with Constantius," John said.

"That again?" Crocus laughed. "You can't be serious."

Sarah had no real argument there, but she felt the need to back up her brother. "I don't know why. Yes, it sounds hard to believe. But you said yourself that the gods sent us, right?"

"I believe Týr sent you to aid me in honoring my father, yes. That is why I think we should attack Marcus now."

"And what if Týr told you to unite with Constantius to accomplish your goal, would you do it?"

Crocus waved his hand at her, dismissing the idea. "That would never happen."

"Crocus." Sarah softened her tone and took Crocus's hand in hers. "It might be the only way John and I can get home. Please, just think about it."

Crocus stared down at his hand in hers, then he looked up into Sarah's eyes. "I don't understand."

"Well, for now, we have to stick together," John

pleaded. "We need your help or we'll die out here."

It was true. They'd been camping and backpacking plenty of times, but only with proper gear, prepared meals, and water filters. Sarah nor her little brother would be able to survive out in this wilderness empty-handed and without help. Sarah made a mental note that to be more independent in the woods, she'd need to sign up for a survival training course.

"I'm very glad to have met you two," Sarah said. "But I just want to go home. And it seems we need your help to do that." She dropped Crocus's hand, trudged over to a rock overlooking the valley, and plopped down.

"I'm sorry," Crocus said. "I can't unite with the man who condoned my father's killing. My father was unarmed and had surrendered, and still that animal Marcus cut him down anyway. I'm not proud that he surrendered, but he didn't deserve to die like that. I must restore my honor by avenging him. It is our way. You may come with us, if you wish. Or—" He swallowed. "This is goodbye."

John crouched next to Sarah. "Come on. Do we have a choice?"

Tears welled in Sarah's eyes, but she blinked them back.

Do we have a choice? echoed in her mind. She was so tired of not having a choice.

"Seems like someone is *forcing* us to, doesn't it?" Sarah asked, a half grin showing to John she was poking fun at herself.

"It's the adventure of it, Sarah. Come on. You love a little adventure, don't you?" John put his hand on her back.

"Adventure, you say?" She cocked an eye at her brother.

"Adventure."

That simple reframing of the situation miraculously struck a chord in Sarah. She was reluctant to ever turn down an offer of adventure. Her brother knew her so well.

She stood and repeated the call. "To adventure!"

CHAPTER NINETEEN

Cliff Jumping

JOHN

John held out a hand to his sister.

She pushed it aside playfully and took off after Crocus and Aurora. John took a deep cleansing lungful of the mountain air, trying to absorb the place, but the breath made him dizzy. He faltered in his step and had to stop, a hand against a tree. Little swirlies jiggled in his vision. His stomach growled, and he massaged it, hoping to rub the hunger away. If he complained again, he suspected it might push Sarah back into a mood, and he didn't want to do that, so he bit his tongue and didn't say anything.

At the end of the lake, a strong stream of frothing water churned from the outlet and went cascading down the mountain. The steep trail—probably nothing more than an animal passage—zigzagged down through a field of large stones and scree. They paralleled the waterfall, a freezing cold spray coating the tips of their eyelashes and sticking to their clothes like dew.

It was cold and dangerous and beautiful all at the same time.

"Baaaa!" Aurora shouted out, skipping from one boulder to the next. She paused and looked back at John, who laughed.

"Little mountain goat," he said. This reminded John of his mom's nickname for him—Little Chef. The thought of her stirred in his gut a sharp pang of homesickness for their kitchen, and her humming, and a hot home-cooked meal.

John's attention was pulled back to the present by Sarah skiing down the trail, knees bent, gliding over the loose scree. She took adventurous risks that made John tense. He didn't want any scars like hers and he didn't want her to get any more either. She'd earned the one on her right temple after colliding with the edge of a picnic table while attempting to jump over it on a skateboard. Unfortunately, the corner of the table had stabbed her under her helmet. Fortunately, it was mostly a glancing blow, and thank goodness it wasn't worse. She could have really—

John gasped. Sarah had gone down hard and was tumbling toward the edge of the cliff, knocking stones loose with her flailing arms in a mini rock slide. John reached out his hand as if he could grab her. She had to stop.

Stop, Sarah, stop yourself.

Then to John's utter horror she went sailing out over the edge and was gone.

CHAPTER TWENTY

Don't Look Down

SARAH

One thing Sarah really loved about skiing double black diamonds was that it forced you to focus single-mindedly on the present. Whatever other thoughts or worries or concerns you had were pushed aside by the adrenaline and the fact that you had to concentrate entirely on the decisions only a split second ahead of you. Or, it wasn't really concentration at all. You just let your instincts take over. Sarah loved the thrill of her body making all the right moves independent of her brain. Why couldn't it be like that all the time, where she knew what to do instinctively?

Swish. She pushed left and imagined jumping over a mogul.

Swoosh. She pushed right and imagined a half-pipe wall looming before her.

Swish. She pushed left and—

The ground came hard. That was one reason she preferred skiing over skateboarding: usually a softer landing and more padding. Snow was more forgiving than pavement, but these sharp rocks hurt even worse. The scree was slippery and her left foot had sped down faster than her right and she'd splayed out like a noob. And now she was tumbling.

The rocks sliced at her arms and pulled at her clothes. She grunted and spit and managed to stop rolling, but the mountain was still sliding underneath her and she couldn't slow down and then—she was weightless.

This can't be good.

Then *WHAM.* Oof, it knocked the wind out of her lungs. Her ribs felt like someone had smacked her with a mallet. But at least she was still feeling. Pain meant she was alive, right?

"Sarah!" It was John yelling from somewhere, but the source was lost on the wind.

She put her hand to her head, half expecting a helmet to be there. Opening her eyes, it appeared as if she were suspended in midair over the valley floor far, far below.

That can't be right.

Sarah looked to her left: cliff face.

She looked to her right: cliff face.

After a second of processing, Sarah realized she was on a narrow outcrop of stone like a diving board perched several thousand feet up a giant vertical rock face. She tilted her head back and looked up to the cliff's edge over which she'd launched.

Then she winced in surprise when a hand suddenly shot into view like a zombie pushing from the grave.

"Grab hold!" Crocus shouted, his face peeking barely over the edge.

Sarah shook the cobwebs from her mind and reached up, but it was too far. She'd have to stand up.

First, she got to her knees, but her body wobbled and her mind kept wanting to take a rest. A gust of wind made her sway. Before it could push her off the perch, she flattened onto her stomach and held on. She licked her lips—so thirsty. Suddenly she became aware of how cold her nose was and how hard it was to swallow. She'd never in her life felt her stomach so empty. She almost didn't feel at all anymore, just numbness. Her head swam, but she managed to get into a crouching position, pressing herself against the cliff face lest she go plummeting into space without a parachute. She imagined herself flapping her arms trying to catch the wind, the birds looking at her like, *What is this kid trying to pull?*

The thought made her giggle inexplicably.

"Sarah, Sarah?!" John kept calling.

"Take my hand!" Crocus yelled.

Sarah knew in the rational part of her mind that this was no time for giggling, but she couldn't help it. She imagined people climbing Mount Everest without oxygen must feel this way when their brain is deprived of its proper nutrients. She guffawed out into the void and then snapped her hand over her mouth and looked around as if she'd been rude in a restaurant. Or maybe it was anxiety, nerves pushing out laughter instead of the alternative breakdown.

The thought steadied her and she took a deep breath in, blew it out, another deep breath in—

"Are you okay? Can you reach me?" Crocus shouted.

—blew it out. When she opened her eyes again, she felt more awake, like she'd been dreaming a second ago. Not calm by any means, but ready to attempt a standing position. The reality of her predicament weighed down.

"I'm oh-okay," she stuttered.

"Can you reach my hand?" Crocus repeated, urgency in his voice. "Quickly." He sounded strained.

That gave Sarah the nudge she needed. Her knees straightened, and she stood, back against the rock wall and nothing but sky in front of her. But she'd done it;

she was up on two legs.

Okay, that wasn't so bad, now to just—

As she was reaching toward Crocus, a sudden gust of wind made her shift her feet, and she wavered, arms spinning to regain balance, tiny stones falling into the abyss.

On her tiptoes, she extended her reach as far as it would go and planted her hand into Crocus's. His viselike grip immediately gave her a shred of comfort. She knew she wasn't safe yet, but his grasp communicated to her that it'd be all right.

"I'm going to pull now," he shouted a second before yanking on her arm. The effect was terrifying. Sarah's feet lifted off the perch and she suddenly wanted to go back down. The ledge wasn't safe, but it was solid ground.

She made the mistake of looking down. Dangling over the drop, the ledge no longer visible to her, the valley below seemed to waver as in a mirage. Her brain couldn't process the distance and for a second she wondered, *How long would I fall?*

Then Crocus heaved again and moved her closer to safety.

Sarah pulled herself up and grabbed onto Crocus's forearm with her other hand. He pulled her torso over the edge, and she pulled her knee up the rest of the way. Crocus grabbed her waist and jerked her up farther. She lay flat on her belly on the cold stones and kissed one. She'd never done that before and the fact that she'd actually kissed the ground made her giggle again. Apparently, people really did get the giggles after almost dying.

Crocus groaned. Sarah was surprised to see he was bare chested. The sight caught her breath in her throat and she coughed in embarrassment. Behind him, John and Aurora held a safety line holding him from going over the edge: one end of his tunic wrapped around a thin and gnarled tree stump. The other was wrapped around his right elbow, his arm crooked to hold it tight without a hand to help. Clearly, it was pinching his blood flow, and his forearm was turning purple, making the scarred end all the more exaggerated. John's face strained from the weight.

Sarah pushed herself to her knees and, arm in arm, helped Crocus back to the trail. They both collapsed and let their breaths pant away the adrenaline. John cheered and let loose a torrent of sentences, but Sarah didn't have the energy to focus on the words. She understood the gist of his sentiment and felt his love. For a moment, she remembered that she didn't feel like she deserved his adoration, but she pushed the bad thought away and smiled instead. She was alive thanks to this group of friends.

Her ribs ached and she winced, holding one hand to

her side.

Crocus ground his teeth while Aurora rubbed his right arm. The blood returning must have felt like vicious pins and needles. Sarah's arms and palms were scraped and scratched, but she wasn't hurt badly. Nothing worse than the crashes while learning to board. Crocus looked away when Sarah pulled up her dress to examine her side. It was red and would surely bruise, but she was all right. No bones sticking out.

"Týr is definitely testing me." Crocus chuckled.

A moment of silence passed.

"Thanks." Sarah smiled and cast a sidelong glance at Crocus. "You saved my life."

Crocus nodded, and they locked eyes for a few moments longer.

CHAPTER TWENTY-ONE

Fire from the Mountain

JOHN

Winter in the Alps was technically a few days away, but as they descended toward the valley John welcomed the change to warmer weather with the lower elevation, though he still hugged the wool blanket tight around his shoulders. They came out on a small strip of plateau that overlooked a village below. John could smell cooking meat wafting up from the hearths, and his mouth instantly watered. He heard the bleat of a sheep.

"So hungry," he let slip.

"We can't go down there," Crocus said from the edge of the tree line. "Too dangerous."

John didn't care. The strong scent of a hot meal

washed over him, and his feet carried him out of the shelter of the forest and toward the trail that led down to the village.

Aurora jumped in front of him, her hand on his chest. "You can't. You'll be taken as a slave. Or worse."

John paused. A warm meal in exchange for being a slave for the rest of his life? Hm, he seriously considered taking the deal.

"Nah," he said aloud, swishing his hand to dismiss the idea.

"We need to rest," Aurora said to Crocus while leading John back to the shadows of the forest.

"We need to eat," Sarah said.

Crocus held up his spear. "Set up camp here. I'll hunt."

"Are we still trying to find your tribe?" John asked.

Crocus paused, sniffed once, then looked around the mountains framing them, considering how to respond. "The trail went cold, but—"

"What?" Sarah snapped. "When were you going to tell us?"

"I didn't think it would matter."

"Wouldn't matter? So what's your plan now?" Sarah huffed. "Why don't we just go down to that village and pretend to be Roman and ask for—"

"I will NEVER," Crocus snarled, "pretend to be Roman. I am Alemanni." He thumped his chest with the stump of his right arm.

"Okay, sorry," Sarah said. "But John and I could go. We could get some food and bring it back here to—"

"Bear!" Aurora interrupted, pointing to the plateau. The animal lumbered close enough that it sent an electric thrill through John and he suddenly felt more awake and ready to run for his life. Fight or flight, with fight obviously not being an option.

"Be still," Crocus said.

The bear reared up on its hind legs and sniffed at the air in their direction.

"*Artio*," Aurora said. "It's a sign, Crocus."

"It is," he replied, smiling at the young girl.

Crocus walked slowly out of the forest with his arms raised, talking in a soothing tone to the bear. He announced his name and thanked Artio for visiting them. The bear yawned and moved its jaw like it was talking back.

Aurora chuckled.

"This is funny?" John asked.

"That bear won't hurt us," Aurora said.

"How can you be so sure it won't attack Crocus?" Sarah had her hands in fists and a concerned look on her face, her stance ready to bolt out to help in a fight.

"Just watch." Aurora crossed her arms.

Crocus waved and told the bear they wouldn't bother it.

The bear sniffed a few more times, then fell back onto all fours and waddled away. Crocus turned back to the group with an easy smile.

"To the Helvetii people of this area," Crocus said, "the bear is Artio, the goddess of wildlife and abundance. She is a positive omen. You show her respect as an equal and she will respect you in return."

Aurora pushed a strand of her orangey-red hair behind her ear, watching the bear now at the other end of the field. "Artio is a sign of good fortune to hunters like Crocus. You're hungry, right?"

"Right!" John exclaimed, eliciting a glance from the bear. It bobbed its nose in the air, grabbing their scent one more time, then went back to its tottering stroll through the meadow.

"I'll be back with meat!" Crocus took off into the forest.

"Wait," Sarah said to Aurora, "he's not hunting that bear, is he?"

Aurora laughed. "No, not today with only a wooden spear. Besides, if he killed Artio, that would definitely earn us the outrage of the Helvetii. If we're lucky, he'll bring us a marmot or a hare."

"Yum," Sarah joked. She laughed, then cringed and held her side.

"How's your bruise?" John asked.

"I'm fine." She didn't look at him. "Just hungry."

"I'll eat anything. I'm starving," John said. "Pancakes with syrup and chocolate sauce sound delicious right now."

"I'd even eat your tilapia barley stew," Sarah quipped.

"Ha." John gave her a playful punch. "I'll be sure to fix it for you when we get home."

Sarah nodded, a longing in her eyes. "Yeah. Not 'if.' *When* we get home."

By the time Crocus returned with two dead animals slung over his shoulder, Aurora and John and Sarah had set up a nice little campsite. They'd cleared an area, built another lean-to shelter, and formed a circle of rocks for a firepit. Aurora stuck a couple of Y-shaped branches on either side of the fire ring where a stick could be laid across as a spit to roast the meat.

While Crocus used the fine edge of a sharp rock to skin and gut the two fat marmots he'd managed to spear, John used the flint to start a fire. It took a few attempts and his hopes waned with the damp kindling, but then Aurora added some dry needles that erupted into flame. John nearly jumped for joy.

"Oh man, I've never wanted to eat marmot more in my life," John said, eyeing the large squirrel-like creatures. He'd seen a few marmots in the Rockies, but the Alps version had a stockier build.

More meat, he thought.

"Like you've *ever* wanted to eat marmot?" Sarah chided.

"Yeah, um . . ."

"These are two big ones," Crocus said. "We'll eat plenty tonight!"

"Thank you, Crocus!" John exclaimed. "Three cheers for Crocus!"

"Woo-hoo!" Sarah added.

Crocus nodded once as if he wasn't used to being thanked for hunting and providing.

Aurora laughed at their exuberance, but John was sincerely giddy. He couldn't wait to eat. He was starved!

Things were looking up. Well, besides the fact that they were trapped in time again. But John didn't want to think about that right now. In fact, he could barely think of anything except the meat slowly spinning over the fire, the gristle popping and the barbecue scent driving him mad.

"Is it ready?" he asked again.

"You've waited this long, just a few more minutes," Crocus answered. The sun had gone down and the cloud cover had sunk all the way to the ground. A thick fog surrounded them in a cocoon of firelight.

John warmed his hands over the crackling coals, tempted to wrench a leg from the animal spinning in front of him, teasing his belly. The flames threw shadows across Crocus's face, his eyes wide, mesmerized by the dancing blaze. John wondered what he was thinking about.

While Crocus stared at the fire, Sarah stared at Crocus, then wondered aloud about the tattoo of *LIV* along his right jawline. "Who's Liv?"

Crocus realized Sarah was speaking to him and did a double take. "Who?"

"Liv, your tattoo." She gestured to his face.

Crocus rubbed his cheek on his shoulder, dropped the poker stick from his hand, and pulled up the fabric of his tunic in a failed attempt to cover his face.

"It's no one."

"You're embarrassed to talk about her?" Sarah prodded.

Crocus scrunched his brow. "It's not a person. It was my number."

"What d'you mean?" John asked, curious to hear it wasn't a name as he and Sarah had suspected.

"After Lingones, where my father was killed by the scar-faced Roman—"

"Marcus," Sarah said.

"Yes, Marcus," Crocus sneered. "I was taken as a slave and sold to a man who bought me for his venator school. He's the one who tattooed me with this number. Fifty-four. I must have been his fifty-fourth purchase."

"Oh, like Roman numerals," Sarah said, realization dawning in her face.

"Huh?" John asked.

Perhaps subconsciously, Crocus raked his dirty fingernails over the tattoo, as if he were trying to scratch it off.

"Oh my, I'm sorry to hear that," Sarah offered.

"It doesn't matter." Crocus picked up his stick and poked at the fire.

John tugged on Sarah's arm. "I don't get it."

"In Roman numerals," Sarah explained, "L stands for fifty. I-V is four. So L-I-V is fifty and four, fifty-four."

"Ohhhhh." John understood it now. He frowned. They'd thought it was a girl. The actual truth was horrible. How could one human being tattoo another human being like cattle? Heck, how could people brand cattle too, come to think of it?

"Not every dominus uses tattoos," Aurora said. "The magistrate did not, for example. But beware the ones who do—they're usually the meanest." She frowned toward Crocus, who seemed eager to talk about something else.

When she'd said "beware," it caught John's ear. Aten had said that word too. *Beware the one named Alex.*

"Hey, have you guys ever heard of someone named Alex?"

The question seemed to startle Sarah.

"Alex?" Aurora rolled her head around, thinking.

"There's Allectus," Crocus said.

"Oh, him, nasty brute." Aurora crinkled her nose. "He's a Roman traitor who has allied with the Franks. They've created all sorts of havoc in Alemannia, killed many of our people. We'd love to see him pay for his crimes."

"A Roman and a traitor," Crocus nearly spit. "Could there be anything worse?"

John thought about whether *Alex* could be *Allectus*. "Hm, sounds like a bad man, but you haven't heard of anyone named Alex, specifically, have you?"

"Well, I've heard legends of a Greek named Alexander the Great, but he lived over six hundred years ago," Aurora replied. "I'm sure there are many Greeks named Alex these days—but why do you ask? Maybe I could narrow it down if I knew that."

John wasn't sure how to respond. "Ah, just someone we were told to watch out for. Another bad guy, I guess."

Aurora sighed. "There are a lot of those, it seems. Bad guys, I mean."

"I think this meat is ready," Crocus announced.

"And there are some good guys too," Sarah added,

glancing at Crocus.

"Dinner!" John exclaimed.

Crocus took the stick poking through the cooked marmot off its perch and held it aside. Steam rose and joined the fog surrounding them.

"Wait, let it cool or you'll burn your mouth," Crocus said, swatting John's hand away.

"You sound like my mother," Sarah chided.

"Very well, here you go." Crocus handed the marmot-on-a-stick to Sarah, then picked up the next raw creature already skewered and placed it over the flames. "Plenty to eat tonight." He grinned contentedly and patted Aurora on the back.

Sarah blew on the meat and pulled at it with her fingers but quickly yanked them away and waved them to cool. "Youch."

Crocus laughed.

Suddenly there were voices not too far away. "Shh!" John hissed.

"What was that?" Sarah whispered.

"Look!" Aurora pointed behind them.

Three small balls of fire bounced in the fog.

"Someone's coming." Crocus was already smothering their fire with dirt. "Get down."

Another ball of fire seemed to emerge directly from the mountain.

"Where are they coming from?" John asked quietly,

lying flat.

"There must be a cave," Crocus whispered. "Be still. They're heading away, so maybe they won't see us."

A parade of torches, or lamps, continued to pop out of the mountain. John counted twelve in all. They marched farther away, disappearing into the fog.

The kids lay still and silent for a full minute more, then Crocus sat up and put his hand to his forehead. He stared at the smothered fire, a thin wisp of smoke still rising from the ashes. "We'd better not risk another fire tonight."

"Phew, that was close," Sarah said.

"Well, at least the meat is cooled down enough now." John held out his hands to Sarah holding the skewer. His stomach rumbled.

"Guess we're all sharing this one," Sarah acknowledged.

Crocus stood and paced. "We're not safe here, so we'll have to keep watch through the night. I'll take first shift."

Shifts? John didn't love that idea, but right now all he could think about was dinner. He wanted to gorge himself on cooked marmot, but he had to temper his hunger to share with everyone. Some was better than none.

The meat was fatty and delicious, and the juice ran down his chin. John wasn't sure he'd call it *delicious* under other circumstances, but at the moment his body absorbed the nutrients like life itself. John felt grateful they had this meat, and for Crocus who'd caught it.

"Thank you, really," he said again to their hunter.

Crocus nodded and took a chomp off the carcass.

Later, bedded down with a full belly, Crocus on watch, John burped and smelled the savory flavor of the critter. "I hope I don't acquire a taste for marmot," he said to Sarah.

"Why do I fear your next recipe?" she joked.

John watched the gray outline of Crocus's shadow in the fog at the edge of their camp, his spear held by his side. He felt warm snuggled with his sister and Aurora, the two blankets spread over the three of them.

A sudden nearby hoot made him stir, and he imagined the scar-faced Roman surprising them and selling them to slavers who tattooed his face with a hot iron, then forced him to battle a fierce lion in the gladiator ring. He shivered the image away.

Sarah pulled the blanket up to his neck. On his side facing away from her, John smiled at the kindness.

The activity of the day weighed on his eyelids and without realizing it, he started humming to himself, lulling his mind into sweet sleep.

CHAPTER TWENTY-TWO

A Mysterious Cave

SARAH

Morning finally arrived. Or close enough. The sun hadn't yet blasted its rays onto Sarah's eyelids, but she'd hardly slept and with the dark night turning gray, she decided she'd had enough of trying. She rubbed her face and yawned. Her mouth was parched, thick with the stench of barbecued wild animal. It made her shudder and sit up, looking for water. Surprisingly, John still snoozed in the blanket, curled next to Aurora. Usually, he was awake before her.

Sarah scanned their campsite, looking for the canteen. It rested against the rock where Crocus had been on watch, but he wasn't there. She looked back to the blankets. He wasn't there either. She hadn't noticed him leave in the night. Maybe she did get some sleep . . .

Perhaps Crocus was just off peeing in the woods?

Then she realized no one had asked her to take a shift on lookout duty in the middle of the night. Did he think she couldn't handle it?

Typical boy, she thought to herself. The notion that he saw himself as her protector made her smirk, and she'd never let him off the hook for not letting her take a turn as his equal in watching over the camp.

She whipped off her blanket and stood, rubbing her eyes and scratching her head. Her hair felt dirty and knotted, and she could only imagine how she must look. She scratched at her scalp and picked out a few pine needles, stretched her back, and took a deep breath. The chill of the air caught up with her and she shivered, but it felt good to be up and moving her tight muscles. A hot shower sounded divine.

Dawn shot into the valley, clear of fog now, and it looked like a part from *The Sound of Music*: towering snowcapped peaks surrounding a huge U-shaped glacier-carved valley like a giant skateboard ramp, the early sun beaming a spotlight on dark birds drifting lazily on the currents.

Smoke rose straight up from the houses in the village nestled near the stream down below—a sign of no wind down there either. Sarah heard the clink of a pot, the bleat of a sheep.

An idyllic place to wake up in nature.

Except this wasn't normal camping. This was sometime in the ancient past and she was nowhere near her home or her parents. The reality fell on her like a ten-ton boulder, and her shoulders slumped from the weight. She scowled.

Aurora stirred and looked around. "Where's Crocus?"

"Crocus?" Sarah snapped, half surprising herself at how irritated she sounded.

"Wha—" John raised his head, strands of his brown hair matted straight up.

"He didn't wake me for lookout," Aurora said, sitting up.

"Me neither," Sarah said.

"Hm," Aurora grunted, her lips pursed.

"I have to pee," John said.

"Then go pee." Sarah gestured off to the trees and rolled her eyes.

John stumbled toward the mountainside.

"Did he tell you where he was going?" Aurora asked.

"He just said he's going to pee."

"Crocus?"

"No, John."

"What about Crocus?"

Sarah shook her head. "Oh, I don't know. He wasn't here when I woke up."

Aurora sprang to her feet, eyes wide. "He wasn't?"

"Noooo . . ." Sarah said. "Should we be worried?"

Aurora whipped her head around, looking for something.

"What are you looking for?" Sarah asked.

"I don't know," Aurora answered. "Some clue about Crocus, I guess. He wouldn't just leave us, so—"

"You think he was—what, kidnapped?"

Aurora put her hand over her mouth. "It doesn't make sense. Why would they only take him?"

John ambled back. "Let's go check out that cave." He pointed to where they'd seen the fire from the mountain in the mist.

"It's too dangerous," Aurora said. "Probably a meeting place for those who follow the mysteries of Mithras. We should get as far away from here as possible. But not without Crocus."

"Come on, please?" John clasped his hands together as in prayer.

For a second, Sarah flashed back to the cave in the Rocky Mountains that took them to ancient Egypt. But unlike in Colorado, this time John was *urging* them to go explore the cave. Previously John had pleaded with her *not* to go, to wait for their parents before spelunking. If only she'd listened—

"No." Sarah crossed her arms. "Aurora said it's too dangerous."

"Well, aren't you Miss Snippy this morning." As soon as John said it, he cringed and backed out of Sarah's reach.

Sarah put up a hand as if she were going to swat him, but it was just a threat. It worked every time, though.

John turned and ran straight for the cave.

"No!" Sarah shouted, running after him. "Stop, Johnny!"

John did stop. But not because of Sarah's order.

"Whoa," John mumbled, his head lolling back as he examined something.

Sarah saw it too. "What is it?"

Aurora had followed them and was now by their side, tugging on their arms. "Stay away. We shouldn't be here." Her eyes darted around. "We need to find Crocus and get out of here. Right. Now."

"Why?" John asked. "What is this place?"

At the top left of the entrance to the cavern was a carving of a man with a flaming crown like the one Sarah had worn in the museum. He was reaching his hand toward another man emerging from the rock, who held a knife at the throat of a bull.

"I remember seeing that before, with the bull . . ." Sarah said.

On the top right was a woman with a crescent moon over her head, driving a chariot.

"The sun and the moon," John murmured.

"We should leave," Aurora urged.

Something about this cave niggled at Sarah's mind. Flanking either side of the doorway into the mountain stood statues of a man with a lion's head and a snake wrapped around his body. Sarah ran her hand over the lion's snout.

"What is this place?" Sarah asked, looking to Aurora. In her mind, she couldn't help but remember the cave that led them to ancient Egypt and the statue of Wadjet. Could this cave be a portal too?

She looked at John, at the pendant of the eye of Ra dangling around his neck.

"You don't understand," Aurora said. "The mysteries of Mithras have a loyal following of Roman legionaries. Legionaries. Do you hear me? So the longer we stay here, the more likely we are to encounter them."

"So that parade of lights last night—"

"Likely soldiers," Aurora said. She stopped tugging. "We really should go."

"But—" Sarah looked to John again. Should they try the pendant here? If it worked, she'd feel bad about abandoning Crocus and Aurora, but—she didn't want to lose their chance if this was it. "Should we try it?"

"Try what?" John asked, but he looked down at his chest where Sarah was staring. "This?" He held up the pendant.

"Tell me more about this place, about Mithras." Sarah looked to Aurora.

"I'll tell you, but not here. And we need to find Crocus."

"No, here. Now," Sarah demanded. Her cheeks flared hot, suddenly. She hadn't meant to snap at Aurora, but based on the surprised look on the girl's face, she obviously had. Ugh, why was she always making people hate her lately?

"Sorry," Sarah said. "Just tell us, please. I think—I think this might be . . . *important*."

"Sarah?" John asked, his head cocked at her. She could tell he was feeling nervous about what might happen next, about what she might decide for them. But she knew he'd go along with it.

Aurora looked down the trail. "Fine, but quickly. And then we go and find Crocus."

"Good," Sarah said, crossing her arms.

"There are many Romans who believe that Mithras was born from a rock, sacrificed a bull in a cave, then feasted with Sol—"

"The sun god," Sarah added.

"Yes."

"Like Sol Invictus, the Unconquered Sun."

John piped in, "Whose birthday is coming up on December twenty-fifth near the winter solstice."

"Yes and yes," Aurora said. She acted impatient, constantly checking behind them down the trail.

"And this?" Sarah pointed to the carving above the opening.

"That is Sol"—Aurora pointed to the man on the left with the flaming crown, which Sarah now realized were the rays of the sun—"and that is Mithras, born from the rock"—she pointed to the man with the knife to the neck of the bull—"and that is Luna in her chariot waiting to take Mithras to the heavens."

Sarah remembered the story about the chariot of Ra, pulled by beams of light.

"Like Ra and Khonsu," John said, excited. "Gods of the sun and the moon. And look at this." He was just inside the cave now. "Here's Mithras eating with Sol."

Aurora huffed in frustration. "Get out of there. We shouldn't be here!"

Sarah had never seen the girl, usually so calm and wise, act so agitated.

"This is a place of sun worship," Sarah muttered to herself. "This has to be another way back, Johnny. It has to be!" She suddenly turned to Aurora and embraced her in a hug.

Aurora was caught surprised, and her hands flailed out. "What are you doing?"

"I'm sorry," Sarah said. "Thank you so much for everything, but I think this is where we say goodbye."

She let go of Aurora and held her at arm's length. "Tell Crocus I— Just tell him thanks, okay? Maybe we'll"—the words stuck in her throat—"meet again. Sometime." She smiled warmly as she stepped past the lip of darkness to stand beside her brother. Could this really be it?

"Uh." John cleared his throat. "Sarah, we can't just leave Aurora here all by herself without Crocus."

Aurora looked thoroughly confused. "You two are so strange." She looked past them into the darkness behind like, *You know you're in a cave, right?*

"You really should go," Sarah said. She imagined the flash taking Aurora with them back to Maryland, as it had transported Zack and Rich and Ella from ancient Egypt to Colorado temporarily. That had been interesting, but she didn't intend to rip Aurora out of her time too.

Aurora huffed an exasperated breath. "That's what I've been saying! We should *all* go."

"Go where?" The voice of Crocus from within the cave made them all jump. John squealed and fumbled the pendant in his hand. Crocus laughed and put up both arms. "Sorry to startle you."

Sarah put her hand to her chest and groaned at him. "You nearly gave me a heart attack."

"You said something about going? Going where?" Crocus repeated.

"What are you doing in here?" Aurora hissed. She entered the cave and tugged at him. "We should get out of here. Now."

"Have patience, Princess, I was just looking for food. They leave offerings to their gods, and I thought we could find some fresh bread from those soldiers last night." Crocus let her pull him along.

"Hey!" A voice from down the trail. Sarah spun to look.

Three Roman legionaries blocked the path and their way out. But Sarah had another idea for how they might escape the cave.

CHAPTER TWENTY-THREE

Not a Fair Fight

JOHN

John's knees shook. This wasn't a museum exhibition or a Renaissance Fair reenactment, and those real weapons looked awfully sharp.

"What are you kids doing up here?" The legionary who spoke had a sloping forehead and rigid brow that shadowed his deep-set eyes. By the way he jutted his face forward, John imagined him squinting at them.

"We mean no harm," Aurora said.

"No harm, huh?" The shadow-eyed man looked to his clean-shaven compatriots, and they all laughed.

"Trace the eye, Johnny," Sarah whispered to John from behind, her hands on his shoulders. The eagerness in her voice urged John to do it now and do it fast. His finger twitched a little, but he started tracing the eyebrow.

Wait. If it worked, they'd take all these people with them. No, he couldn't do it right now. But maybe if they could get farther into the cave and away from the soldiers, they could bring Crocus and Aurora with them just like they'd brought Zack and Rich and Ella back too.

"Do it!" Sarah hissed.

"Hey there, easy," said the shadow-eyed legionary. He held his sword in his right hand and with his left, a bronze cuff around his forearm, he patted the air as if the kids were wild animals. He crouched forward carefully, like they might bite or run off.

Given their last few nights, John did feel sort of wild, actually.

Sarah gripped his shoulders tighter, the tea kettle of her patience boiling over in the space of a breath. John knew right away it was because he had hesitated when she commanded he act. She spun him around, grabbed the necklace and pulled it closer, yanking John by the neck. "I'll do it," she sneered.

"Stop!" the legionary cried.

But Sarah had already traced the eye.

And nothing happened.

"You have to do it!" she screamed, her right fist tight and shaking in the air next to John's face.

"Sarah!" John barked, but cowering as he said it, afraid of her wrath. "I don't like it when you yell at me." He could feel tears behind his eyes, but he wouldn't let them come now, in front of all these people, in front of Sarah.

"Look," John said, holding the pendant up with his finger on the edge of the eyebrow. "I'm doing it. I'm tracing the eye like you want."

His finger went around the almond-shaped eye, down the line with the curlicue end, then up and down the line with the knifelike edge. "There," he said. "I did it. I'm doing it." He traced it again and again. Nothing every time. His eyes were on Sarah, watching her watching his finger like a hypnotized cobra. He'd been so focused on giving his sister her way that it hadn't even occurred to him that there was no flash of bright light.

But there was no flash, no white searing bolt that transported them through time and space. The realization made him stop his finger.

"Enough!" The shadow-eyed legionary boomed so forcefully that John shook from the blast, stifling his breath.

"They're the slaves that escaped Aventicum," the smallest legionary said, pointing with his sword.

Something dawned on the second man now too. "The reward. Caesar Constantius offers a reward for two Gallic slaves disguised as Romans, and two Alemanni slaves. Two girls. And two boys, one with no hand—"

They eyed John, who had both hands in front of him.

"You," said the shadow-eyed man, pointing at Crocus. "Let me see your hands."

Crocus kept his arms tucked into his tunic.

The soldier advanced. "I said . . . let me see your hands." His tone was like a low growl.

The soldier suddenly stopped, his eyes wide and looking up the mountainside. From inside the cave, John couldn't see what had grabbed his attention, but the sinister legionary suddenly seemed afraid, backing up.

John heard the low growl again, except this time he realized it hadn't come from the soldier. It was something outside on top of the cave.

Something big. The bear?

John looked up as a streak of dark fur arced over the entrance from the earth above, like a storm rolling through the air toward the soldiers.

Terror struck the legionaries, and they faltered backward but remarkably regained their footing and stood their ground, their training and instinct kicking in.

The wolf landed between the kids inside the cave and the legionaries blocking the path. It growled and snapped its jaws and when it looked back, John noticed a white patch of fur between its eyes.

"Sarah—" John said, pointing to the wolf that she had helped to save its pup.

Sarah smiled and put her fist to her mouth. She coughed a single laugh, smiling at the wolf.

Crocus and Aurora had their jaws wide open in astonishment.

The soldiers swung their swords and advanced. The wolf growled and made lunging challenges, looking for an opening to attack, but their blades made it near impossible.

Suddenly a rock sailed out of the cave and thudded into the chest of the shortest soldier on their right. John looked over at Crocus, who was bent over picking up another stone. He did the same.

The soldier had been caught off guard, and the wolf took advantage of the split second, pouncing her weight into the man and taking him down to the ground. Its jaws exploded open, and it went in for the bite, but a sword nicked its haunch and it recoiled. The two standing legionaries slashed and encircled their fallen comrade, pushing the wolf closer to the edge of the cliff.

"We have you now, beast," the shadow-eyed man said.

"She is sent by Týr, Roman scum!" Crocus screamed,

hurling another stone.

"Yeah, leave her alone!" John shouted. He chucked his rock too. It caught the shadow-eyed leader in the face and split his chin open.

The man snarled and clutched at his wound.

The wolf attacked. As he collided with the middle legionary her wicked bite locked on to the man's shoulder. The shadow-eyed leader stabbed with his sword and pierced the wolf in the paw. The animal whimpered in pain and again retreated back to the lip of the cliff, limping. Its hind leg skittered, knocking gravel over the edge of the drop.

Sarah let loose a terrifying plea. "Nooo!" This was a cry of anguish and fear, the likes of which John had never experienced and a frightening bloodcurdling wail he hoped he'd never hear again. The veins in her neck popped and her face blared beet red. She moved to run to the wolf, but Crocus held her back. She beat at his chest, but he held her tight, tears streaming down her cheeks.

Aurora stood in front of her and tried to catch her eye.

The soldiers couldn't help but give Sarah their momentary attention. Their heads bobbed back and forth between Sarah and the wolf, not wanting to let either out of their sight.

The wolf replied to Sarah's howl with one of her

own. Sarah joined in, harmonizing with the wolf that echoed far into the valley.

"It's witchcraft!" the smallest soldier blared, obviously frightened at the bond between Sarah and the wolf.

John couldn't help it. He joined in the howl too. A moment later, Crocus and Aurora did the same, amplifying the effect.

"Enough!" shouted the shadow-eyed legionary. "She's not a witch, she's just a child."

With the wolf no longer guarding the entrance to the cave, and itself in danger of being pushed over the edge of the plateau, the soldiers had the upper hand, no matter how strong the rallying cry the kids and the wolf had made together. The man who'd been bitten in the shoulder stood up, blood dripping out of his sleeve, but he still held his sword.

"You two get the slaves while I end this beast." The shadow-eyed legionary twirled his weapon. The wolf set her feet, ready for the one-on-one sparring to begin.

The other two soldiers approached the cave.

Off to his right, John suddenly heard more yelling, the sound of men's deep voices like war cries and the sound of drumming steel on wood. The three soldiers heard it too and looked up the plateau. From their angle in the cave, John couldn't see who was approaching, but it sounded like an army.

"We need more men!" the smallest one pleaded to their leader. "There's too many."

The shadow-eyed legionary sighed. "Retreat."

"And them?" The middle soldier looked at the kids, then let his sword drop and held his shoulder with the other hand. John wondered if the soldier was much older than Crocus, if at all.

Their leader growled at his defeat. "They'll slow us down. Just grab the little girl and let's go. Hurry!"

The middle soldier jogged toward Aurora, who stood her ground without an ounce of fear showing. Her worry seemed locked away behind an iron facade.

"No!" Crocus put himself in front of Aurora.

"Come on. Move!" With a grimace of pain, the soldier raised his sword again, then looked at whatever horde was approaching on the plateau. "Or I'll have to poke you with the pointy end of this thing. Move it!"

"No, Constantius wants them alive," the leader ordered.

"There's no time—they're upon us!" The small soldier fled, running down the trail.

With his captor distracted, the wolf took its cue and bolted past the shadow-eyed man. Even with the limp, she still sprung lightly and as swift as the wind. The legionary swung his sword, but it only swooshed through the air, missing its target.

The sudden movement of the wolf startled the

soldier about to slash Crocus, obviously more afraid of the wild animal than some unarmed kids. While he was distracted, Crocus kicked straight forward into the man's chest, sending him tumbling backward down the trail in a puff of dust.

Sarah ran out of the cave and watched the wolf go. John reached for her, worried for her safety with the legionary so close, but the soldier wasn't paying her any attention, instead gritting his teeth and waving his sword at whoever was approaching. Then the shadow-eyed man took off running after his fellow soldiers.

The wolf and the legionaries gone, Sarah turned around to face whatever new challenge approached on the plateau.

John stepped from the cave next to his sister, not sure what he'd see. Were they simply swapping one enemy for another? Were the Helvetii coming to attack them as invaders?

One worry just replaced another.

He grabbed for Sarah's hand and she accepted it. The group of savage-looking bearded men stopped their charging run and walked toward them. They carried spears and swords and shields and their faces were painted with blue streaks, some with hair matted in dreadlocks. Others wore a knot on their head like Crocus.

Aurora stood firm, but John couldn't tell if it was

from bravado or that same iron facade she'd portrayed to the Roman legionaries.

The tribe stopped about ten feet away, their faces showing no hints of emotion, their musky odor wafting across the divide. The leader was huge, with a heavy fur cloak and bear claws on each of his shoulders that made his bulk seem all the greater.

"You," the hulking man said, glaring at Crocus. "I ought to cut you down for what happened."

Crocus didn't respond. Aurora's eyes snapped from the tribal leader to Crocus, then back again. The breeze whisked their hair and if John hadn't known better, he could have imagined a tumbleweed blowing by and the stereotypical whistle announcing a Wild West-style showdown.

Crocus's stare never wavered from the man challenging him.

The bear man's hand hovered over the sword sheathed at his side as he stepped forward into the gap between the two groups. Crocus stepped forward to meet him, the man towering above Crocus and twice his width. It was like a giant tree shading a sapling.

The quiet added to the tension. John needed to pee again.

Then the huge man burst into a loud guffaw of laughter, threw his arms wide and wrapped them around Crocus, pulling him in tight for a bear hug.

Aurora laughed too, like she'd just been holding it in and knew how the standoff would end all along.

John breathed out, finally. "What was that?"

"Oh, he's a big softie, but he likes to keep you wondering," Aurora said.

"Who is he?" Sarah asked.

"That's Alaric!"

CHAPTER TWENTY-FOUR

Everyone Deserves a Break

SARAH

Sarah wasn't sure she could trust the dirty bearded barbarian called Alaric. He looked like some sort of pro wrestler. Right off the bat, he'd teased and taunted Crocus, and though he played it off as friendly, it came across more like a bully. Crocus didn't seem to mind, smiling broadly, and Aurora ran to Alaric with arms outstretched for a hug. But still, there was something not right about this man with the claws of a bear on his shoulders.

"What'd he mean about 'what happened'?" Sarah leaned to John and whispered.

John's eyes were wide surveying all the different tribesmen.

"Don't you wonder?" Sarah repeated.

"What?" John blinked and looked at her. "This is amazing. It's like a living history display at the museum."

"I wonder what *happened*. Maybe it's about how they were separated from the tribe in the first place," Sarah said.

"He was joking around," John replied, waving his hand toward the group hugging and backslapping.

Sarah wasn't convinced. There was history there.

"Sarah, John, come meet Alaric." Aurora waved them over.

Alaric pulled his lips tight under a jumble of snarled beard and looked the kids over. "I'm told you talk to wolves."

"Nice to meet you too," Sarah said.

"I'm John." He waved. "Are you their dad?" He gestured to Crocus and Aurora.

Alaric laughed. "No, but Aurora is my niece."

Aurora looked at Crocus. "And he's not my brother. He's my protector, appointed by my father the—"

"That's enough!" Crocus clapped his hand over her mouth. "I watch out for her, that's all. Been watching out for her since she was a wee child."

Why had Crocus interrupted? Sarah wondered.

"Not always that easy, is it?" Alaric winked.

Crocus sighed. "About that—"

"Don't worry about it. I'm glad you're both safe," Alaric said, pulling Aurora into the bear fur of his cloak and patting Crocus on the shoulder. He looked down at Aurora. "Your father will be glad to see you again, little P."

Aurora cast her eyes down, as if guilty.

"We should return immediately to the North," Alaric declared loudly.

"You can't go yet!" John said, looking to Crocus.

"And why not?" Alaric peered down his nose at John. Sarah understood what John was getting at: their quest. If they went north, how would they unite Constantius and Crocus? Wait, was this guy "Alex," the one Aten said to beware? Alaric, Alex? Maybe Alex wasn't some obvious bad guy but someone who would unknowingly stand in their way like Alaric was about to do now.

Sarah's eyes tilted up at the tall man before her. Alaric certainly commanded obedience by his mere presence. He was definitely the leader here, and Crocus would no doubt follow his orders. But how could she get Crocus to turn against his tribe? Was that even fair to ask of him?

Sarah had no idea *why* Aten had asked her and John to unite Constantius and Crocus, so how could she convey that to Crocus? Well, he had said *grave danger* if they didn't, but that wasn't very specific. Sarah needed to understand more about what Aten had said.

"I need to think," Sarah said, hand to her temple. She turned her back on the group and took a step away before John grabbed her by the elbow.

Not now, Johnny, please. Give me a dang minute to myself for once.

"Sarah, wait," John said.

"Don't yell at me, John!" Sarah yelled, not recognizing the irony. As soon as it escaped her lips, she clipped her mouth shut. John hadn't been yelling. The stress of the situation compounded with lack of sleep and her own wanting to live up to the standards of a good older sister, to guide her brother safely home, it just—it felt like too much sometimes. She needed a break.

Suddenly she realized they were watching her. She looked to Crocus first.

His pale blue eyes conveyed genuine concern. "Sarah . . . I know."

Know what?

He continued, taking a step toward her with his hand out. "I know this isn't your family and you miss yours." Okay, not too far off. "But we'll help keep you safe. On my honor." He stiffened his back and thumped his chest with his stump.

Aurora stepped beside him and made the same gesture, clenching her fist and holding it to her heart.

"Me too," John added, stepping beside Aurora. He looked like a goofball with his puppy-dog smile, compared to the stoic pledge of allegiance from the other two. Sarah giggled at him. She rolled her eyes and shook her head.

They all meant well, but Sarah knew they couldn't solve her problems or do her thinking for her. She wanted a few minutes to herself. Well, really, she wanted to go home.

Aurora stretched a sad look at Sarah, as if she could read her mind and sense her conflict.

"I'm sorry," Sarah muttered. She didn't know what else to say and she knew that further talking would only make it worse. Touched by their kind act of solidarity, Sarah didn't feel worthy of such love. The guilt of getting her brother mixed up in all this in the first place reared its head, made all the more confusing by their wanting to protect her. She didn't need protection! She didn't need anyone.

They were probably better off without her. She opened her mouth but shut it again quickly.

Ugh. Sarah knew she'd ruin this moment if she said anything, but she couldn't look at them anymore, so she turned around and walked off down the trail.

CHAPTER TWENTY-FIVE

Captured

JOHN

John knew Sarah needed some time to gather her thoughts, but she'd really been stalking off to be by herself more and more often lately. He worried about her and wanted to give her the space she wanted. And yet, he didn't want to be apart from her. They couldn't separate now, he knew that much. Not now, not ever.

"Sarah, wait," Aurora shouted. She started to go after Sarah, but John held her back.

"I'll get her," John said. "In a minute. She just needs some time."

"Let her go." Crocus put his hand on Aurora's shoulder.

"It's too dangerous," Aurora reminded him.

Crocus clenched his jaw and looked up after Sarah. She had already disappeared down the trail.

"We're going to head back up the mountain," Alaric said. "You can do whatever you want, Crocus. But you"—he pointed at Aurora—"we've been searching for you. You're coming with us, little P. You're too important to risk another minute in this occupied territory." He turned and conferred in hushed tones with another tribesman.

Crocus swallowed and looked at John. Then he stared down the trail and licked his lips as if the next thing was hard for him to say. "Goodbye, Sarah."

"What?" Aurora shot him the stink eye. "You can't give up on her that easy!"

"I'm *not* giving up on her!" Crocus snapped in an uncharacteristic outburst. "You heard Alaric. It's not up to me. And what can I do for her, anyway?"

John grinned. "We need you and I have this funny feeling—you'll need us too."

"What d'you mean?"

"You know what I mean."

"Not that Constantius business again," Crocus huffed.

"Constantius?" Alaric turned back to John. "What about that invader?"

John averted his eyes from Alaric's hateful stare. He wasn't trying to defend the Roman caesar of Gaul, but he knew—knew what? *Then the world as you know it is in grave danger.* That sounded pretty important.

He had to talk to Sarah. She'd know what to do. He backed away, unable to think of an appropriate response. If they left without him and Sarah—no, he couldn't let them do that. He'd have to catch Sarah and bring her back to the group before they got too far away. John ran.

"I'm coming with you," Aurora said, jogging after John. "They won't leave without me."

They caught up with Sarah as the trail intersected a larger road. To their right, it curved out of sight and down to the village. To the left, the road wound up into the valley beyond. Again, the panoramic view distracted John for a moment.

"Just leave me alone for once, John." Sarah's shoulders slumped and she sagged onto a boulder. Then softer: "Just leave me alone. You're better off that way." Her glance flitted up to John for a second and then down again.

Aurora sat next to her and said nothing.

"Sarah, you know that's not true," John said. "Look, we have to go now if we want to stick with Crocus and accomplish our mission. I'm scared, Sarah. I don't know how it makes any sense, but Aten said 'grave danger,' Sarah. Grave danger! That doesn't sound good and I don't think we should ignore—"

His words were cut short by the sound of a group coming up the road around the blind turn.

As John looked to the corner, the scar-faced Roman appeared high on a horse, beside him the soldier wearing the lion's head and carrying the golden eagle staff with the red flag, and behind them a large group of Roman legionaries extending around the curve.

"Halt!" Marcus shouted. John was already frozen to his spot at the sight of the army. "Seize them!"

Aurora bolted first, but an arrow appeared suddenly in the ground inches from her feet and she lost her balance to avoid it, tumbling to the ground in a cloud of dust.

"Aurora!" Sarah yelled and ran to her.

Legionaries surrounded them before John knew what had happened. Sarah and Aurora stood beside him, John's hand reaching out and finding his sister's. They both squeezed.

"Are we gonna get out of this one?" John asked.

"See, you wouldn't be in this mess if it weren't for me," Sarah said, her feet shuffling nervously.

"We always do," John said. "Say it. We always do."

"I don't know, Johnny." Sarah's eyes were glassy, their normal shine dulled.

John heard a warbling bird and thought, despite the circumstances, how lovely it sounded. He'd heard it before, at the house from which they'd rescued Aurora.

He heard it again and recognized it as Crocus's familiar call. In the line of trees above them, Crocus waved to Aurora, who must have seen him after the first calling trill.

"Sarah, look," John said.

Sarah raised her eyes to the tree line as Crocus turned his back on them and disappeared.

Sarah snorted.

The Romans used a coarse rope to bind John's hands, then Sarah's and Aurora's. They were tied together and ordered to march.

As they turned to descend, a whiz of arrows flew down around them. The soldier holding Aurora's rope fell to the ground with a shaft sticking from his neck.

"Cover and defend!" Marcus rallied, his sword held high in the air. "Protect the prisoners!"

Someone shoved a shield over John's head.

Battle cries and charging Alemanni exploded from the forest. The tribe, led by Alaric and Crocus howling at the front, flew toward the Roman army.

"Shield wall!" Marcus barked. "Take the prisoners away now!"

The rope tying John to Sarah and Aurora yanked them down the trail and John stumbled. Behind him, he heard the clash of steel and the painful cries of wounded men as a great battle raged.

The Romans led them at a jogging pace down the

road toward the village.

Aurora kept glancing back, though they were out of sight of the skirmish.

"Keep up back there," one said to John, pushing into his back with a shield.

"Where—are you taking us?" Sarah asked in between breaths as they marched in double time.

"Back where you belong, slave."

CHAPTER TWENTY-SIX

Non Nobis Solum

SARAH

In the small village at the base of the mountain, the Roman legionaries loaded Sarah, John, and Aurora into a cart pulled by two large black horses. They took off at a gallop. Other riders accompanied them, in front and behind their wagon, a royal parade of sorts. Sarah tried to comfort her brother, but they weren't allowed to touch or to speak. When she tried, the soldier watching her smacked her with a club. Helpless, she stared through a space between the slats of the wagon at the rushing cobblestones underneath. A tear streaked down her dirty cheek.

Aurora returned to her stoic iron facade, not a tear nor an ounce of fear. Sarah considered herself a pretty brave girl, but Aurora was in a class by herself.

When they arrived back in Aventicum, they stopped near the arena where Sarah, John, and Lucas had magically appeared. A gruff man with two missing front teeth hauled John away despite Sarah's sorrowful pleas, despite John's sheer terror. One threat of a backhand and John cowered, going along with the man but never taking his eyes off Sarah as he disappeared into the darkness of a stone tunnel.

Separated. Alone. Maybe forever. Tears rimming her eyes, Sarah glanced at Aurora. Well, with Aurora still here, she wasn't quite alone but without her brother her heart ached a loneliness she'd never felt before. A hole where something that was always there was suddenly gone. She'd taken him for granted. Was Aurora thinking about Crocus in the same way? It was hard to tell.

Was their quest doomed and she'd live out the rest of her days separated from her family and trapped in time?

Her own words echoed with guilt in her head: *Just leave me alone for once, John.*

She snorted and the tears fell. *Careful what you wish for.* Right then and there, she resolved never to say those words again to her little brother. If they ever saw each other again.

These thoughts ran on an endless repeat in her mind

until the cart halted in front of the magistrate's house. Sarah recognized the carving of Mithras on the arched entryway to the villa.

The magistrate welcomed Sarah and Aurora to his home as the sun was setting. "She was a good slave," he told the guards. "Until she ran away." He clucked his tongue. *Tsk-tsk.*

"Would you like this one too?" the Roman soldier asked, poking Sarah in the back. She couldn't help but step forward, closer to the old man. He wore a clean white sheet wrapped around his thin frame, more like a toga than a tunic. The wrinkles in his face formed deep valleys sagging from his chin and large pockets under his eyes.

"A gift from Marcus for the trouble caused by the younger one."

"Oh, that's very kind of him." He turned to Sarah: "Open your mouth."

Sarah didn't respond or acknowledge in any way. She felt like a flat tire, useless.

The legionary held the club aloft, dark against the sky.

"Hold." The magistrate put up his hand. "She will obey."

"What—What have you done with my brother?" Sarah asked in almost a whisper. Her lips were dry and cracked.

"You have a brother?" the magistrate said.

"John," Sarah said. Then she wrung her hands together as if in prayer. "Please. Please don't hurt him."

The magistrate looked to the soldier expectantly.

"He is *damnati ad ludum venatorium*."

"Oh, how exciting," the magistrate said, clapping his hands together. "He'll battle the beasts for Caesar!"

"No . . ." Sarah's lip trembled.

"Look at the bright side," the guard said. "Maybe he'll win his freedom."

Was that supposed to be helpful?

"Come," the magistrate said. "I'll take care of you. I'm about the best you can get around here. Isn't that right, Aurora?"

"Yes, Dominus," Aurora said, her head down. Then to Sarah: "He did treat me well, Sarah, considering."

"What does it matter?" Sarah said.

"Now, open your mouth," the magistrate said.

Aurora nodded once, and Sarah found herself opening her mouth. It felt like a violation to be treated like a horse at the auction. It felt like surrender.

"Wow, your teeth are immaculate. I've never seen anything like it in all my years. Come"—the magistrate pulled the soldier over—"look at this. So white and straight."

Sarah thought of the braces she'd endured.

The soldier peered into Sarah's mouth reluctantly.

"Yes, sir. White and straight. May I go now, sir?"

"Yes, yes, thank you." The magistrate pulled a small pouch from within the folds of his clothing, then handed a few coins to the legionary.

The soldier walked across the courtyard and under the archway carved with *Non Nobis Solum*.

"Not for ourselves alone," Sarah muttered. "Ha." She rolled her eyes.

"Oh, legionary!" the magistrate called. "One more thing."

"Sir?" The man snapped to attention.

"When is her brother scheduled to appear in the arena?"

"Tomorrow afternoon, sir."

"Thank you."

"Sir." The soldier gave a short bow and left.

Tomorrow afternoon? So soon? Sarah cringed. John had only a day to live.

The next morning, Sarah was supposed to be learning from Aurora all the chores she'd have to do as a slave.

"Seriously?!" she said to Aurora as the girl showed her how to tromp barefoot in the tub with all the wet laundry.

"To get the dirt out," Aurora said, as if it were a silly

question.

"While John's life is on the line, I'm doing laundry?"

When Sarah was nine, her parents told her she would start washing her own clothes. At the time, it seemed like a fun thing to load the machine, and she liked the feeling of responsibility. But with repetition came boredom and then it became a chore. At least she didn't have to stomp on her dirty clothes in a tub full of water in bare feet. If she and John could get home safely—no, *when* they got home safely—she'd never complain about laundry again.

"Sarah, don't worry," Aurora said. "I'm sure Crocus is plotting with Alaric right now. They'll get us out."

"And John?"

Aurora paused, then nodded. "I'll make sure of it." That sounded like quite a presumptuous claim from a nine-year-old girl. But the way she said it, and the way she looked Sarah in the eye when she did, Sarah believed her. She smiled.

A male slave interrupted. "The dominus wishes you join him for lunch."

Sarah and Aurora looked at each other, then followed the man into the dining hall, a room with a high domed ceiling lined with tiny tiles that formed a beautiful pastoral landscape.

"I know, I know, slaves eating at my table." The magistrate threw his hands up like he'd been caught guilty. "Just don't tell anyone, okay?" He smiled warmly. "It's not something you should get used to, but when I welcome new servants into my home, I like to dine with them. I view you as human, but make no mistake that you are still my property. Do we have an understanding?"

The bile rose in Sarah's throat and her stomach flip-flopped. She couldn't fathom how owning a human being was ever considered okay.

Aurora nudged her.

"I said," the magistrate reiterated, "do we have an understanding? I will treat you well, as long as you do the same to me and your fellow servants. Isn't that right, Aurelius?" He looked to the slave who had summoned them to lunch.

"Quite right, Dominus." Aurelius bowed his head slightly in a sign of respect.

"Agreed," Aurora said.

"And you?" The magistrate waited for Sarah to answer.

Did she have a choice? *Blech*, that thought made her want to spit. She'd groaned and felt trapped in her life before, but this put it into a completely different perspective. Maybe she'd had more choice than she thought.

"Agreed," she whispered. She wanted to wash her own mouth out with soap.

"And per our customs, since I am your owner, you will address me as Dominus. Agreed?"

Sarah swallowed. "Agreed, Dominus."

"Wonderful." He smiled a toothy grin. "Now let's eat."

They sat down to lunch. Aurelius and another girl brought in trays filled with grapes, olives, fresh-baked bread, fish, and cheese. The sight of all the food faded the severity of Sarah's situation for a few blissful moments, and she ate ravenously.

"Wonderful," the magistrate said when they'd finished the meal, clapping his hands. "Bring in the libum cheesecakes, please, Aurelius."

Each cake about the size of a bun rested on a bay leaf, a warm golden honey drizzled over the browned tops. The cakes were dense but flavorful. Sarah ate two of them and sat back in her chair, overstuffed.

Considering the exotic meal on which she'd gorged, she thought of John. Their mom called him "Little Chef" because he enjoyed helping out in the kitchen. Right now she wanted so badly to share this libum and honey with him.

"John would love this," Sarah said to Aurora.

Aurora half smiled.

"If he is victorious in the arena, he will be rewarded," the magistrate said, "and have plenty of coin to buy his own dessert. Or if the editor—who will be our illustrious Caesar Constantius today—feels he fought bravely, he may even grant him the *rudis*."

"Rudis?" Sarah asked.

"It's a wooden sword," Aurora filled in, "a symbol, granted to a fighter who wins his *manumission*." When she saw Sarah's confused look, she added, "His freedom."

"Have you never been to the games?" the magistrate asked.

"So if John fights bravely, he could be freed?" As soon as Sarah said it, she heard the hope in her voice falter at *bravely*.

Sarah had a hard time picturing that for John in a fight with real weapons against real wild animals. He did have his brave moments—like the time he jumped over those scorpions in ancient Egypt—but battling ferocious animals in the ring did not sound like a fair fight.

"And when can *we* be freed?" Sarah asked.

The magistrate laughed. "Oh, my dear, as you can see"—he waved his arm around the opulent dining room, the art decorating the walls, the feast before them—"I have no need to sell you."

"So how long are we here?" Sarah looked at Aurora. Aurora looked awkwardly at the magistrate, who chuckled.

"She doesn't want to say it. How polite. You are

mine until my death, dear. However, if you serve me well, when I die I *may* choose to grant your freedom. I have no heirs, so if you serve me well, you might be freed then. But"—he waved to Aurelius in the corner to serve more dessert—"let us enjoy our time together until then."

Sarah could feel the steam roiling inside of her. This was impossible, ridiculous, a person couldn't be owned!

"Come, dear," the man said. "Look at me. I'm an old man. It might not be that long. You are wiser to be polite and earn your freedom while you still can."

"Not for ourselves alone, huh?" Sarah snipped. "Seems like all you care about is yourself."

"I'm sorry?" the magistrate responded.

"Me too." Sarah sat, stewing, unsure of what she would do next.

The magistrate watched her, then picked up his fork and continued with the second helping of his dessert.

"I'm done here." Sarah pushed her chair out in a huff.

"You may go," the magistrate said, "and finish the laundry."

"Me too," Aurora chimed in.

The magistrate nodded, and Sarah heard Aurora's pattering feet follow her out of the dining hall.

Sarah turned a corner.

"This isn't the way to the laundry," Aurora said, confused.

"I'm not doing this old man's dirty laundry."

"Oh?"

"I'm going to the arena. I have to save John."

Aurora stopped. "If they catch us, they may not be so kind again."

Sarah stopped and looked back. "Then stay. I'm not asking you to go."

The hurt look on Aurora's face gave Sarah pause. "I'm sorry, I—"

"You're not asking her to go where?" Aurelius stepped into the hall, his hands behind his back. He was tall and lean, his head cocked up slightly as if he was looking down his nose at them.

"Nothing, uh—" Sarah stammered. "I was asking her where the bathroom is."

"Well, which is it?" Aurelius cocked an eyebrow. "Nothing? Or do you need the latrine?"

"I—I—"

"I'll show her." Aurora grabbed Sarah's arm and pulled her backward.

Aurelius shot his eyes sideways toward the dining hall where they could hear the distant clink of the magistrate's fork on his plate. "That's not the way."

Aurora continued to tug at Sarah, but Sarah yanked her arm free. "What d'you mean?"

Aurelius held his finger to his lips in the universal sign of "*shh.*"

Sarah narrowed her eyes. What was this guy's deal?

Aurelius tilted his finger away from his lips and pointed to the kitchen. "I hear"—he winked—"that you can get out through the kitchen window, which is unlocked and unbarred. If you stand on the sill, you can lean out and pull yourself right up to the top of the courtyard wall."

"Why are you telling us this?" Sarah asked, squinting.

"I've been with the magistrate since I was your age." He looked maybe early twenties, so he'd been here ten years? "And I used to take the occasional vacation as well."

"Why are you telling us this?" Sarah asked, still not knowing whether to believe him. Would he go turn them in right after they parted ways?

"One thing I've learned is that living here as a servant at the magistrate's villa," Aurelius said, "is much better than living poor out there. I am enticed to stay not because of the stick but because of the carrot. Or libum cheesecakes, as it may be." He winked again. "You will take care to learn this too, but I understand the need to roam a little. The magistrate will be going for his afternoon rest after lunch and before the games. That gives you an hour or so to go play. Be back before then, so he's none the wiser. Promise?"

Sarah and Aurora looked at each other. Sarah had no intention of making any sort of promise to this stranger. "Promise."

"Good, now hurry."

Sarah and Aurora moved toward the kitchen. Behind them, they heard Aurelius say, "Have fun!"

CHAPTER TWENTY-SEVEN

Venatores

JOHN

Along with the other slaves, the gruff man with two missing front teeth led John through the same stone archway that he'd used to escape out of the arena right after they magically arrived in this time and place. They were ordered to sit on stone benches lining the hall. John leaned on his spear with both hands and looked up at the sharp tip. It didn't seem real. Sitting in the half dark, back where he had started, John replayed everything that had happened to bring him to this point—Crocus, Aurora, the story of Fenrir and the wolf pup, the scar-faced Roman, the cave of Mithras, the soldiers, the wolf, Alaric, being separated from Sarah— the memories bounced around in his mind like a yearbook in a blender. But mostly, he thought about Sarah. If he'd done something differently, would they still be together? He leaned over and put a hand to his head.

"Nervous?" the person next to him asked, pounding the end of his own spear into the dirt.

John flinched. He'd trudged behind this boy and had wondered if he might be the same age because they were about the same height. Another ten-year-old? The bright whites of the boy's eyes floated amid his dark black skin. In the dimly lit hallway, the effect was mesmerizing.

"Are you nervous?" the boy asked again. "I was nervous my first games too."

"Nervous?" John repeated the question. "I have no idea what I am right now. I've never seen the games." John cocked his head. *Games.* What an innocent-sounding name for such a terrible sport. "We're just kids."

The boy looked him over with disdain. "I'm a man. I'm fifteen."

Fifteen? A man? "Uh, sorry."

"Never seen the games? Where are you from?"

John thought about that a second. "Well, I'm from Colorado, but now I live in Maryland."

"I don't know those places."

"Yeah, well, where are you from?"

The boy—uh, man?—sighed but lifted his head with pride when he responded. "I am Nubian, from the Kingdom of Kush, the city of Meroë."

"I've never heard of that place either, so I guess we're even. I'm John."

"Silko, son of Arakamani." He chuckled. "No, not the king from centuries ago." The line sounded like it'd been delivered many times.

John gave a slight chuckle, pretending he knew what Silko was joking about. "Course. So, where is Meroë?"

"Far from here on the Nile in the south." Silko looked wistfully at the ceiling, as if he was imagining his hometown. "But the city has had many problems and invaders and I don't know if there's even a place for me there now."

"I've been to the Nile in Egypt," John said. "But that was a loooong time ago." Literally, by a few thousand years.

"I miss the dark waters," Silko said. John thought of his own home in Maryland, how much closer they were to the ocean now.

Silence passed between them.

"So what are ya in for?" John tried the old joke about being locked up together. "Murder?"

Silko clenched his jaw and pursed his lips.

Oh! John wanted to slink away, but he didn't want to alert Silko to his unease. And there was someone on the other side of him squished on the bench that was probably also a murderer. And it's not like he had anywhere to go anyway! So John sat still, not sure what to say or not to say.

"I didn't do it," Silko said, obviously understanding John's sudden fidget. "I saw someone—a Roman with a scar across his face—strangling a soldier in an alley. I tried to run, but he arrested me and charged me with the crime. No one will listen." Silko's head flopped back and forth. "No one will listen." His eye and cheek twitched, the anger yearning to break free.

"I-I'm sorry," John said, nearly speechless at the boy's tragic entrapment, but also at the mention of the scar-faced Roman. *Marcus.* "I believe you."

Silko's cheek stopped trembling. "You do?"

John nodded. "I do."

Silko grinned, just barely. "Thank you."

A wave of whispers rushed down the hall.

"Here they come, look." Silko pointed to where a line of warriors approached. "We're just the warm-up act for the real gladiators."

"Who's that?" John asked, nodding toward a thin man with a net and a trident. He had a long gash across his side that wasn't fully healed.

"I don't know his name, but I suspect this will be his last battle. He's a *retiarius*, the fisherman." Silko pointed. "But I cheer for the *secutor* who he is usually paired against." The secutor carried the same short sword and tall rectangular shield that John had seen the legionary soldiers wield. Around his arms he wore thick wrappings and a metal shin-guard-like thing protecting one leg. His helmet fully covered his face with two small eye slits. It reminded John of the helmet Crocus had worn when they first met him.

"Is that a woman?" John pointed to the only gladiator with a breastplate. The bronze was heavily scratched and dented. She carried a short curved sword and a small rectangular shield and bounced lightly back and forth on the balls of her feet.

"That is Ostia. She fights as one of the Thracian and is quite efficient with that *sica* blade."

John did a double take at one of the massive men, the biggest of the group, his arms like tree trunks. The giant walked by, and John noticed his ear had a chunk missing so it looked pointed, as if he were elvish.

No, it couldn't be. John shielded his face by pretending to scratch at his forehead.

The commander with two missing front teeth consulted a scroll and started rattling off the order of the fighters and who they'd be paired up against. "And finally we'll have Lucius. Looks like the caesar is saving the best for last." His mouth went wide in a wicked grin.

In acknowledgment, the giant with the elvish ear

grunted and pounded on his chest. Some of the other gladiators grumbled at being passed over as "the best."

Lucius. It was *Lucas*, the escaped prison felon who had traveled back in time with them, the man who had tried to steal the pendant and had knocked Aten unconscious in the museum. John remembered Lucas surrounded by legionaries as they fled the arena what seemed like a thousand years ago. Huh. Lucas had survived.

"I thought he was dead," John mumbled. He felt for the necklace under his tunic.

"Who?" Silko asked, then followed John's stare. "Oh, Lucius? He's newer than some, but he's never lost yet. Glad we don't have to fight him. I'd rather die by lion."

John didn't laugh.

"You're up first, venatores!" the commander hollered. "On your feet!"

At that moment, Lucius looked over, and John swore the big man did a double take when his scan passed John. John averted his eyes and scratched at his forehead.

The ten hunters stood with their spears held straight up by their sides. They had no armor, no shields, just the clothes on their backs and a long pointed stabbing weapon against angry wild animals.

John's legs barely held him upright.

"You've never been out there." Silko pointed toward

the sunlight and the open arena. The thrum of the crowd mixed with the roar of a lion who didn't sound happy to be there. A high-pitched yipping howl floated in from an animal John didn't recognize. Silko's nostrils flared as he inhaled deeply. "But we're venatores. We fight the beasts to win our freedom." Was he convincing John or himself?

"This is not real," John said. It couldn't be. His palms sweat on the wooden shaft of the spear.

He glanced back and saw Lucius leaning from the line, staring straight at him.

Silko slapped his flat hand into John's chest. It startled him, and he jerked, but he could see it was meant as a friendly gesture.

"We'll have a better chance if we stick together," Silko said, looking John in the eye. "Together, okay? That's how we'll get through this."

I doubt it. The knot in John's throat stuck.

The roar of the lion sent shivers down John's spine. He wanted to run away, but he couldn't think straight. He looked down at his legs moving forward on autopilot with the rest of the line, Silko right behind him and nudging him forward. Their spears bobbed as they marched.

As soon as they hit the bright oval of the arena, the crowd went wild. The lion flashed its menacing fangs, a thick chain around its neck looped through a bolt in the ground, held by a team of six slaves, each wearing nothing more than a cloth wrapped around their waist. No armor, no protection if the lion were to turn on them. They could loosen or tighten the chain to give the lion more room to play. Right now, the beast was held back while the crowd admired its dinner—namely, John and the others. In a cage next to the lion prowled two hyenas with heavy iron collars tied to each other. One yipped, and it sounded like a wicked cackling laugh. The other joined in.

A rhinoceros bucked its horn, rattling the whole cage that didn't look strong enough to contain it. The rhino had no collar, nothing to control the huge creature. A man outside the cage poked and prodded the rhino into a rage to the relish of the crowd.

A lion, two hyenas, and a rhinoceros. And a bloodthirsty mob.

John spun. The crowd chanted. At the end of the arena, a man stared toward him. John held his hand up to his brow against the sunlight.

In his own suite, Caesar Constantius clapped, staring straight at John with no expression. He wore a toga lined with purple and gold, a crown of laurel capping his head.

Then something inside of John, a feeling he couldn't ignore, tugged his focus away from the emperor, forcing him to rotate and face the center of the arena. As soon as he did, an overwhelming feeling of déjà vu flooded him—that feeling that he'd lived this before. Yes, he'd been in this ring when the eye of Ra transported them here—but this was different. He felt like he'd actually lived this before.

He had the undeniable urge to step forward, toward the center of the ring, toward the location they'd first arrived in this time. The crowd receded in his awareness, their cheering dulled. As he moved, it was like he'd made these same steps before in a dream. Toward the center of the ring. Toward where they'd magically appeared. The strange feeling grew stronger and John dropped his spear, reaching his hand to his neck.

"The pendant," he muttered to himself. He took it out of his shirt and turned it to the sun. The jade seemed to glow from within, a fire he'd never noticed before.

"It was here," he said. "It was here that we arrived and it's from here that we can leave."

John thought back to the trip to ancient Egypt. Of course! The eye of Ra they'd traced to escape had been the same one that had brought them there—in the same location. The portal didn't move. They arrived at this exact spot and so they could only leave from this exact spot. He'd done it, he'd figured out the secret to getting home! He simply had to trace the pendant in the same place they'd arrived.

His finger moved to the brow of the eye of Ra. He was going home. This was the way. He knew it to be true without the shadow of a doubt, and the thrill made him laugh out loud while the crowd cheered. He was going home! What a show he'd put on for them now!

John's finger sparked with static electricity as he traced it over the brow, around the almond eye, down the line with the curlicue finish. Then only the line with the knifelike edge remained, and he'd be gone with a flash. This was definitely it. He shut his eyes.

Sarah's face filled his vision. His sister. He couldn't leave without her. His eyes snapped open, and he dropped the pendant like it was a spider. It dangled from around his neck.

The volume of the crowd suddenly boomed back to normal.

The rhinoceros thrashed against its cage. The lion roared, straining at its chain. The hyenas jostled and yanked at their collars chained together, making them all the more frenzied.

"My fellow Romans. Your attention, please!" the announcer yelled from a podium in the stands, waving his arms. "We have a change to our schedule and a special treat for our illustrious caesar Constantius who has so kindly gifted us with these games." The crowd clapped and whistled.

Constantius waved in different directions, acknowledging their adoration.

The announcer patted the air with his palms for the crowd to let him speak. "One of our finest newcomers to the gladiator stage has requested he join the venatores this afternoon!"

The crowd hushed.

The gate to the exit rose.

"I give you . . . the gladiator Luciussssss!" The announcer drew out the name as would a boxing ringmaster. The crowd stood and stamped their feet, creating a booming roar. Women in the front row threw flowers. The lion snarled and gnashed its teeth.

Out walked Lucius. He now wore an ornate bronze helmet with an arc of metal across the top, out of which sprang horse hair like a Mohawk. He carried a small round shield and a large sword, wielding the heavy weapon with ease.

Lucius's helmet was staring straight at John, and his stride aimed directly on a collision course.

"Pick up your spear, John!" It was Silko shouting. "Here comes the lion!"

John looked over his shoulder at the lion racing

toward them. It slashed at the first venator, who dove to the ground. The lion pounced on top of him and opened its jaws to bite, but Lucius ran forward and pierced the lion's side with his sword, diverting the lion's attention and saving the fallen hunter.

"That's good!" Silko beamed. "Stick together! Help each other and we'll win. Together!" He shook his spear.

Suddenly a flash of gray nearly rammed into the lion but collided with Lucius instead, knocking him through the air. The rhinoceros had been let loose. The lion leapt onto the back of the rhino, digging its claws into the thick hide. The rhino spun and bucked. The six slaves holding the lion's chain were dragged forward in the sand, their ropy muscles struggling to contain the beast.

The crowd cheered. John wanted to shake every person in the mob. How could they think such cruelty was entertainment?

The hyenas streaked toward the downed venator as the easier prey. Slobber hung from their jowls, their ribs visible on skinny frames. John scowled. These animals were obviously starving and crazed.

Lucius wobbled to all fours and shook his head.

The venator on his back in the sand rolled to his spear and brought it up in the nick of time, skewering the first hyena in the shoulder. It yelped and recoiled.

The second hyena was nearly jerked off its feet by the tug from the collar on its thick neck. The venator jabbed again, the hyena narrowly dodging the sharp thrust.

The sting of the spear only served to enrage the first hyena. It wheeled around and bit into the venator's leg and dragged him, flopping around like a rag doll. The second hyena grabbed hold of the venator's other leg and whipped his head back and forth like a shark does to tear its catch.

Silko whooped a battle cry and ran toward the hyena, his spear held out in front of him in a charge.

The lion had dropped from the rhinoceros, who was now blindly stampeding toward the guards who held the chain for the lion. They dropped their hold on the lion and went skittering behind a protective wall that didn't look strong enough to withstand a charging rhino. The lion was now free, dragging its chain loose behind it.

John's body vibrated with fear and adrenaline. He stepped back and looked around. If he didn't do something, he'd be lion food in a matter of minutes. Could he run? The gate to the exit had been closed.

Maybe he should trace the eye of Ra and save himself. He could come back for Sarah. Right? *Right?!* *Hurry, John, think.*

Silko lanced one of the hyenas dragging the venator,

and it turned to face Silko. The second hyena stepped next to his twin, and they both bared their teeth in a growl. The wounded venator clawed at the ground, trying to pull himself away, but he was badly hurt.

The rhino collided with the wall of the arena in an explosion of dust and mortar, then the animal stood still as if stunned. Lucius was on his feet and staring at John again.

The hyenas both took a menacing step toward Silko, their heads lowered and ears back in attack position, the hair on their backs standing straight up.

John rushed toward Silko. "Silko!"

He'd get to Silko, trace the eye of Ra, and save them both from these poor animals and from Lucius. He'd come back for Sarah. He would. He'd come back. Sweat dripped into his eyes as his legs pumped.

John skidded to a stop behind Silko. The Nubian boy held his spear tight, holding off the hyenas, his eyes locked on the approaching threat.

Now, John. Trace it now. Or you'll never have the chance.

The hyenas pounced simultaneously.

Silko fell backward, knocking John down too. John dropped the pendant from his grasp.

John punched and kicked at the hyena on top of him, the snapping jaws only inches from his face, the foul breath making his eyes water, drool dripping onto his cheek. The raging animal opened its mouth wide, and

John landed a fist squarely on its snout. It crinkled its face and whimpered. In the split second while the hyena shook it off, John reached for his spear and pulled it alongside the animal's bony rib cage. It tore at the flesh, and the animal screeched, backing away.

Lucius appeared and kicked the first hyena off Silko while slashing at the second that John had injured. His sword met the animal's skull, and it flopped over dead. The remaining hyena scrambled away, lugging its fallen twin by the collar.

"Thank you!" Silko stood and held up his fist and spear to Lucius in solidarity. "Together!"

"Move." Lucius pushed Silko aside and held his sword tip at John's neck. Then in a hoarse growl, he said, "Give me the necklace."

Tilting his head down to look at his own chest, half not believing the necklace was still there, John knew he couldn't hand it over. It was their only ticket out of this mess. However, a sword makes a compelling argument.

John moved to unclasp the necklace, his fingers trembling. But he stopped when, suddenly, Lucius looked toward Constantius and his body tensed. Something was wrong.

John followed his gaze. A troop of brightly outfitted Roman legionaries surrounded Constantius and rushed him out of the theater. The rhinoceros turned and bucked its horn. The hyenas had both been felled, a few of the venatores standing over them with their spears raised in triumph. The lion stalked toward the group of hunters, but the slaves had emerged from their secure enclave and reclaimed the chain.

"Ladies and gentlemen," the announcer called out, "if you'll please leave the arena in an orderly fashion, we've been ordered to evacuate. All soldiers report to the eastern gate."

The crowd sat silent for a moment, then chaos broke out like wildfire.

Lucius looked at John and growled. "Now! Give it to me or I'll take it."

John eyed the open exit gate behind Lucius, then the gleaming blade at his throat.

The slaves were reeling the lion back to its cage.

"We're under attack!" someone screamed from the arched hallway.

Lucius looked back.

On impulse, John rolled from under Lucas's stance and was on his feet before Lucius even noticed.

"No!" Lucius cried. John heard the swish of the sword much too close and he bolted away. Silko jumped up and ran with him. John had no idea how he'd escape, but he had to get away from Lucius. Maybe once he was clear, he could trace the eye and—

Cries burst from the crowd, adding to the chaos. A

real fire had erupted and was crawling up one of the overhanging awnings that provided shade, quickly racing across the tinder-dry fabric and sending a plume of smoke into the arena.

John did not look back to see if Lucius was in pursuit, but the ten-foot-high wall of the arena was closing fast. He had no idea how he'd get out, but something told him he could fly right up it at this moment, if he wanted to. He'd—

His vision suddenly sparked white. Thunderbolts of pain shot throughout his head as he flung forward, mashing his chin into his chest and catapulting him forward into the sand.

John blinked repeatedly, but the world was fading around him like the end of a movie. His head hurt so bad and he wanted to lift his hand to feel what had clobbered him. He wanted to stand up and keep running, but he couldn't move. He couldn't will his legs or his arms to move.

As his vision narrowed, he swore he heard Sarah calling his name. It couldn't be real, but he smiled.

Then someone lifted his head onto what felt like a cushion, and he realized he must be dreaming. He looked up at his sister, felt her cool hand on his cheek, her head blocking the sun like an eclipse. A smoky breeze spread her red hair like the rays of the sun on the crown of Sol Invictus.

CHAPTER TWENTY-EIGHT

Left for Dead

SARAH

When everyone else in the crowd panicked and ran *up* the stairs to get out of the arena dug into the earth, Sarah ran *down* the stone steps toward John. She knew Aurora was following her, but she focused instead on getting to her brother.

John took off sprinting away from Lucius and toward the wall nearest to her. She shouted to him, but he couldn't hear her. There was too much chaos, and her voice couldn't cut through the noise. The smoke from a fire in the stands made her cough.

"Watch out!" Aurora cried, pointing at Lucius.

The man everyone called Lucius, who she knew as Lucas, threw his small shield like a discus and it soared through the air, colliding with John's skull and sending him face-planting into the dirt.

Sarah howled for her brother and leapt down into the ring, landing safely in the sand next to John.

"No, Johnny, no," she begged, falling to her knees. She rolled him over onto his back and pulled him onto her lap. The back of his head was damp with blood.

Sarah wept while she stroked his cheek.

"Give me the necklace!" Lucius boomed, stomping toward them.

Sarah couldn't respond, her face buried in John's chest, hugging him close, willing him with every ounce of her strength to wake up. "Wake up, Johnny. We'll get through this like we always do, right?" She rocked.

"Princess!" It was Alaric, running across the arena from the arched hallway.

Sarah looked up at him. *Princess?* She realized he wasn't talking to her, but to Aurora in the stands. Crocus and the rest of the army charged behind him shouting like a raucous barbarian horde.

Lucius turned and saw he was outnumbered. He looked back at John, cradled in Sarah's arms, then shouted, "It's mine!" and started running toward the necklace.

An arrow suddenly burst through Lucius's side and made him stagger. He snarled and snapped off the shaft. As he turned, Crocus landed a forward kick to his wound that sent him down into the sand. Multiple Alemanni threatened Lucius to stay down with their weapons. Some with swords, others with bows pulled taut. Lucius growled.

Alaric rushed past them and put his hands up to Aurora. "Thank Týr you're safe. Stay there. We'll come to you."

"Not without them," Aurora said, pointing to Sarah and John.

"Princess, legionaries approach," Alaric said, waving his hand back to the open gate.

Sarah looked up at Aurora through the smoke, through her tears.

"I demand it," Aurora said, crossing her arms.

Alaric growled.

"As you wish," Alaric snipped.

"Hurry!" Crocus grabbed Sarah by the elbow and yanked her to her feet.

"No!" Sarah kicked and flailed. "Don't leave John!"

"We're not!" Crocus replied. Then he shouted to a bald, bare-chested tribesman while pointing at John: "Get him. Quickly!"

The bald man picked John up and flopped him over his shoulder.

Several Alemanni ran to the wall and bent over with their hands on their knees. Another tribesman then used them as a stool to stand and reach the lip of the wall. They pulled themselves up and over, then helped the next man up and out of the arena into the stands.

Alaric handed Sarah up the chain, her eyes on John.

Just then, the familiar rattling of well-armored Roman legionaries entered the arena from the arched hallway. They greatly outnumbered the Alemanni.

The Romans assembled into a line and were practically hidden behind their large, rectangular shields. The tips of long spears jutted out over the top edge of the shield wall as they advanced at a steady pace. Another group of Romans formed behind the shield wall. These were archers. They notched arrows into their bows and awaited orders.

"We need to leave now," Alaric barked to his men. "Hurry!"

The tribesman guarding Lucius backed away and ran to the wall. Arrows thunked into the ground around them. Lucius stood, unarmed but holding his side where he'd been pierced by the arrow, and ran toward the bald man carrying John.

The bald man held John as high up on the wall as he could. An Alemanni at the top reached down, but just then an arrow punctured the bald man's chest, and he fell as if an imaginary string holding him up had been severed. John dropped into the sand as Lucius neared.

"John!" Sarah screamed, her hand reaching for her brother as an Alemanni warrior carried her up the stairs and away from John.

Alaric swung his sword at Lucius to keep him back.

"I just want the boy," Lucius boomed.

Alaric looked to the approaching Roman army. Sarah knew he couldn't fight both. She knew that something very bad was about to happen.

Alaric left John where he lay and jumped up the wall.

Lucius bent down toward John and ripped the necklace from around his neck. A look of enchantment came over him, like he didn't even care about the blitzing arrows or the approaching Roman army.

"We can't leave him!" Crocus yelled.

An arrow landed in Alaric's calf, and he cried out in pain, nearly falling over. Another arrow thwacked into the shield hanging on his back.

"There's no choice. Help me up!" Alaric shouted. Crocus leaned down and grabbed Alaric. Several other tribesmen assisted in hoisting Alaric up the wall. An Alemanni with dreadlocks groaned and slumped over into the arena, an arrow protruding from his head. He landed with a thud next to John and didn't move.

The Roman legionaries arrived and were thrusting their spears dangerously close.

Lucius had disappeared behind the shield wall. With the necklace.

"Aurora," Sarah shouted, "we have to save John!"

"I know," she replied. "I know." She said it softly and did not issue any commands. An arrow sailed over Sarah's head, and she didn't even duck instinctively.

"We must protect the princess!" Alaric yelled, glancing back at the Romans. His men fled up the stone steps. Alaric limped with the arrow still sticking out of his calf, his arm draped over the shoulders of a fellow tribesman. Alemanni bowmen covering them from above let loose a barrage of arrows that thunked into the shields of the legionaries. One toppled backward, his absence leaving a hole in the shield wall.

The Romans had overrun where John lay helpless.

"John," Sarah cried, barely a whimper. They were nearly to the top of the stands and out of the arena.

Crocus stood on a bench, facing the army. The Romans were crawling up the wall and Crocus needed to run, quickly, but he was staying behind. For John? Sarah held hope like a dying flame.

Crocus pointed his sword at the centurion down in the arena. "Your time will come, Marcus!"

The scar-faced Roman stood firm, staring right back at Crocus. "I'll be waiting." His lip sneered into a scowl.

With arrows whizzing all around and the legionaries pouring into the stands like ants, Crocus turned and ran.

CHAPTER TWENTY-NINE

A Scout Brings News

SARAH

The Alemanni escaped the town and fled to a nearby forest, where they disappeared. Sarah assumed it was only a matter of time before the Romans would come after them, but she didn't care. She couldn't believe they'd left her brother behind. This was not happening. This was definitely not happening. If John was . . . No, she couldn't bear to think it.

Sarah felt an emptiness in her gut that was unlike any hunger. She thought of those snail shells you find on the beach, hollow and vacant and only a vague hint that something once lived there.

Aurora sat down next to her on the log. "Was he—gone—when you held him?"

Sarah wiped her eyes. "No." She turned her whole body to face Aurora. "No, he was still alive. We have to go back for him."

"Alaric wants to get me home," Aurora said, her head down and feet scuffling in the grass like she was ashamed to say it.

"Who are you, anyway?" Sarah asked. "A princess?"

Aurora sighed. "No one is supposed to know but, yes, I am the daughter of the chieftain of our tribe. Alaric made a mistake by calling me that in the arena. He's a brave warrior but not the wisest of our clan. If Constantius finds out, I'm sure he'd love to take me as a hostage to use as leverage against my people."

"That's why he called you little P. For Princess," Sarah said.

"I hate being called that." Aurora glared. "That sort of thing is part of the reason I ran away in the first place. I'm tired of not being able to make my own choices. My father is always training me for my 'big responsibility,' he calls it. But what if I don't want it?"

Sarah chuckled. "I know how you feel."

"You're a princess?"

"Well, no, but—"

"I do love my tribe, but sometimes I yearn for—"

"Freedom," Sarah finished her sentence.

"I was going to say independence, but yes." Aurora smiled. "I'm tired of everyone treating me differently.

Just because I happened to be born to a certain family at a certain time and place, I don't think that makes me any more special than you or John. Or anyone. We should all be treated as a piece of the whole. The mountain is the less without every rock."

"Wow, well said. The forest is the less without every tree."

Aurora chuckled. "That is what I like about you and John. You treat me like any other kid." Aurora gazed out through the forest. Sarah imagined she was thinking about John.

The lump in Sarah's throat bulged. "Why don't we go back for my brother?"

"We will." A tense silence passed between them. Aurora searched in Sarah's eyes. "But it won't be easy." She took Sarah's hand. "I convinced Alaric to send a scout to find out about John. Wait until we hear that news. Will you?"

"You sent a scout?"

"Yes, he left already."

Sarah pulled her hand away and stood, scanning the forest. "When will he be back?"

"As soon as he knows the answer to whether John lives."

They spent several excruciating hours waiting in the forest, but later that night the scout returned. Alaric and Crocus were not pleased with Aurora for requesting the scout, and they made it clear that it endangered them all to send a man back into town. The fact that the Romans never deployed an army to find them made Alaric all the more nervous. It was unlike the Romans not to seek blood, he said. They must be scheming something.

The Alemanni scout was a wiry man, a thin warrior whose skin held tight against his tattooed cheekbones, the narrow beard jutting from his chin giving him a long face. He was built like a runner, Sarah thought. Thin, but strong. An endurance athlete.

His news made Sarah overjoyed and terrified.

John was alive but a prisoner in the emperor's personal villa near the arena, heavily guarded at all times by a troop of soldiers led by a scar-faced Roman.

"We have to go get him!" Sarah pleaded in the firelight.

"Alaric," Aurora said, "we owe it to Sarah to save her brother."

Alaric laughed. "We owe this girl nothing, little P. I told you we'd send a scout, and that was dangerous enough. But we're outnumbered against the army holed up behind those defenses. It would be no contest."

"That's not the brave warrior I know," Aurora teased. "And let me tell you of this girl's kindness and bravery to change your mind about whether we might owe her something. It was her selflessness that saved my life and Crocus's."

Sarah was taken aback. She wouldn't exactly describe herself as selfless. Brave? She tried, sure. Kind? She could do better. But selfless?

While Aurora described how Sarah had saved the trapped wolf pup and how that same wolf had saved them from the Romans at the cave of the mysteries of Mithras, Sarah's mind wandered instead farther back in her own past.

She'd acted selfishly when exploring that cave that took them to ancient Egypt, ignoring her brother's more levelheaded pleas. She knew it wasn't her fault they'd stumbled upon a magic time-traveling portal, and yet she harbored a guilty conscience because going into the cave, against John's urging, had been the first domino that started all this mess. And so she kicked herself: it was her selfishness that got John into this situation that almost killed him. She blamed herself alone.

Non Nobis Solum. Not for ourselves alone. The Latin phrase they'd seen inscribed in the arch of the magistrate's house flashed into her mind. At home, she had been shunning John a little more lately. It wasn't his fault she felt bad about everything. It made her irritable to have no one to confide in about her shame, but it was her own embarrassment that prevented her from reaching out, if she really admitted it. It was so hard to apologize and seek forgiveness.

One time she'd overheard her dad apologize to her mom. When her mom smiled and accepted it, they hugged close and her dad said, "Thank you. Being forgiven and accepted is one of the best feelings in the world."

Forgiven and accepted. Sounded nice. So why was it so hard to apologize?

"It's true," Crocus said. "We would have been captured by those Romans if it weren't for that wolf, if it weren't for Sarah's bravery. She also saved us when guards were chasing us by chariot."

Sarah blushed. His praise supporting her felt like a warm blanket on a cold night.

Alaric grunted and stared into the fire. Some of the men chewed on their dinner or drank or sharpened their weapons. The fire crackled.

"Besides," Crocus added, "I want another shot at the scar-faced Roman for the death of my father."

Alaric looked up from the fire at Crocus and took him in for a moment. "For Val." His head bobbed as if contemplating his decision. He stood, an ax in his fist, and eyed his men, who stopped their chewing and drinking. The sound of whisking rock on metal ceased.

Everyone stared at Alaric. The fire threw shadows up his tall body and into his beard. The bear claws on his shoulders seemed to be twitching.

"For Val! Father of Crocus and brave Alemanni warrior who died with honor at Lingones! For all our fallen fathers and brothers and sons!" Alaric shouted, raising his ax into the air and shaking it at the night sky.

The men cheered. "For Val!"

"For Val!" Crocus joined in the chant.

"For John," Sarah said quietly. "Here we come, Johnny. Just hold on."

Crocus leaned over to Sarah. "See, I told you."

"Told me what?"

"You were sent by Týr to help me avenge my father's death. He sent us that wolf pup in distress as a test. You showed your bravery, and now he is rewarding you with the fiercest warriors in all of Alemannia to save your brother."

The chanting died down, and the men returned to their eating, drinking, and weapon sharpening.

Alaric's eyes were wide with the thrill of a group call to battle. He immediately started planning with Crocus. "We attack at dawn. The eastern gate is nearest but will be more heavily guarded, since that is where we penetrated last. To attack from the north, we'd have to go by water but we have no boats. That leaves the west or the south. What do you know of those approaches?"

"There is a main road to the south that leads all the way to Rome over the Great Pass in the mountains, so I'd expect heavier traffic that way," Crocus said. "The way west also has a road, but it leads out to the territory of the Franks."

"The Franks," Alaric sneered. He spit into the fire. "No doubt the way west is heavily fortified."

"Why wait until the morning?" Aurora said.

Both men looked at her.

"Leave this to us, little P," Alaric dismissed her.

"Why not sneak in tonight? They'll least expect it," Aurora said. "That is how I escaped Crocus's 'protection' when I ran away. I just waited until he was asleep." Aurora poked him in the ribs, teasing.

"Don't remind me," Crocus groaned.

"The watch towers are manned at night too, dear Princess." Alaric didn't actually roll his eyes, but Sarah could hear the sentiment.

"Stop calling me that," Aurora scolded. "I don't wish to hear that name again."

Alaric rolled his hand in the air in a mocking gesture of royalty. "As you wish, dear . . . niece."

"Tonight is their Dies Natalis Solis Invicti. While they celebrate their sun god, we come from the north, but we don't go to the docks by boat because they are guarded," Aurora said.

"How then do we enter?" Crocus asked, as if she were a silly child.

"Through the aqueducts. The Romans have built a beautiful stone system for transporting water." Aurora let it sit for a second before continuing. "They have tunnels that run underground big enough for a man to walk through. Though you may have to duck, Alaric." She smiled at her uncle. "We find one that channels the lake water into the town and follow that past the main gate."

Alaric snorted. "I'm sure it'll be blocked by its own gate, Prin— It'll be blocked too." He looked to Crocus for support.

Crocus smiled. "Of course, but it won't be guarded. We pry open the bars enough to enter the tunnel, then slip into the city unnoticed. Very stealthy. You have the cunning mind of a chieftain's daughter." He winked.

"The scout can lead us to the home of Constantius," Sarah piped in. "For John."

"Yes," Crocus agreed. "For John. And the scar-faced Roman. Two for one."

Coming on the wind from the Alps, Sarah could swear she heard the distinct victorious howl of a wolf who'd caught its prey.

CHAPTER THIRTY

To Meet an Emperor

JOHN

John's head still ached, but the pain and swelling had subsided. He'd been tended to by an old man who claimed to be Constantius's personal physician.

The kind, elderly doctor had gently rubbed the salve from an aloe plant on the back of John's head where he'd been clobbered by Lucius's shield. John was surprised to learn that the aloe plant stunk of onion—nothing like the zesty smell of the lotions he'd used on sunburns—but the soothing relief felt like a natural cold compress all the same. The healer brought him a tea that smelled sharply of strong peppermint mixed with chamomile and lavender, with tiny chunks of what looked like brown tree bark. After a mug full of that and a fresh application of aloe, John had relaxed and fallen naturally asleep. He realized he needed the sleep, as if he hadn't slept in a week. Thoughts of his sister and his mission tried to invade his thoughts, but his brain had had enough and shut down.

Later that evening, he awoke with a start, snapped his eyelids open, and put his hand to his face. No more beads of sweat on his forehead. He felt more like himself again. He wiggled his fingers and his toes. He lay there conducting an inventory of himself when in walked a girl with tight braids. She carried a long-necked jug with a handle on either side like the amphorae that Lucius had thrown at Aten back in the museum.

Sarah. John wondered where she was, if she was with Crocus and Aurora. A vision from a dream floated through his memory where Sarah was holding him in her lap and looking down at him, her red hair radiating like a crown.

"Good evening. Glad to see you're up," the girl said, smiling. Pouring some water into a bowl, she added, "Fresh from the aqueduct. Thirsty?"

"What day is it?" John asked, his throat dry. He accepted the mug of water from the girl.

She laughed. "You've only been here a few hours. It is still the birthday of the Unconquered Sun." She beamed a big smile.

"Dies Natalis Solis Invicti," John murmured, remembering what Aurora had told him. "That's what you call it, right?"

"Yes." There was a kindness in her eyes. "My children really enjoyed the chariot races. I can't believe in the final that Cyrus beat out Octavius. It was so close, and Cyrus was the underdog! Don't you love it when the outsider wins like that?!"

John did a double take. This girl didn't look old enough to have one child, let alone plural *children*. "You have kids?"

She giggled. "Oh, they're not mine, but, you know, the ones I care for."

Oh.

"The caesar requested that you join him for dinner," she said. "I told him I'd check on you, and here you are: awake and alive." Her bubbling energy was contagious and made John grin without realizing it. She continued, "Your clothes are there. I hope you don't mind I washed them for you. I've never seen undergarments like—" She paused and looked away, her cheeks turning pink. "And, uh, your shoes. Such delicate craftsmanship. How long have you been here from Greece?"

John could barely keep up with her rapid-fire effervescence. Maybe he did have head trauma. "Greece?"

"Yeah, you worship the Greek goddess of victory, Nike. Though I've never seen her represented by that red shape like a . . . Hm."

"A swoosh."

"A swoosh," she repeated, smiling. She said it again, exaggerating the vowels. "Swooooosh. I like that word." She shook her head at him. "You are one of the caesar's strangest guests, if I may be so bold to say. I mean that as a compliment."

John couldn't wipe the silly grin from his face.

"Anyway, I'll leave you some privacy, but call me if you need anything." She disappeared out the doorway. The guard in the hall nodded to her as she left, then returned his steely gaze back to the captive, his hand on the door.

John swung his legs over the side of the bed and realized he was naked, the bedsheet still covering his midsection.

"Oh, and don't forget," the girl said, swinging her head back around the door frame. John scrunched more of the sheet over his body to make sure he was fully covered. "Dining hall in thirty minutes."

"Yeah, uh, okay, thank you." John tried to act cool, but his face felt hot.

The girl giggled and disappeared again. The door closed. John wrapped the sheet around his waist and stood.

On a nearby footstool made of white stone sat his clothes—his shorts, Denver Nuggets T-shirt, tunic, and ankle socks. On top of those rested the eye of Ra amulet on its leather cord. John picked it up and rubbed his hand over the smooth jade.

He had to find Sarah.

"Hello." The emperor greeted John with a tight smile and gestured for him to sit at the chair diagonal at the table. The man's lips seemed too small for his broad angular jaw. His pinched forehead bulged on either side in a Y-shape down to ears snug against his head. He had short-cropped hair and a stubbly thick chin that jutted out almost the same length of his nose. Overall, the impression made him look both athletic and as if he were pained, as if he were straining to hold in flatulence. "Do you know who I am?"

"You're Constantius," John offered.

"That is my name, yes. But more than that, I am one of the four co-emperors in the Tetrarchy of Diocletian, charged with maintaining law and order in the region of Gaul for our great Roman Empire."

"I'm John, charged with—uh, not much."

"Uh-huh." Constantius picked up his napkin and set it in his lap without taking his eyes from John. "I invited you here, to my personal residence, because I believe you are special, John."

"Special?" The slaves brought out plates of meat, purple carrots, cabbage, and mushrooms. In the center of the table steamed a freshly baked loaf of golden brown bread. John tore a hunk and shoved it in his mouth. He realized he was starving.

"Very special," Constantius said. He had his elbows on the table and his hands clasped in front of him, as if in prayer, watching John eat. He picked up his utensils and asked casually, "Tell me about that necklace."

A mushroom stuck in John's throat and he choked. Constantius paused his cutting and watched John hack. "Was it something I said?"

"No," John managed to say. He took a drink from the cup in front of him, but the acrid taste of alcohol made him spit.

"You don't like our wine?" Constantius asked, his pinched forehead squeezing tighter.

"No, it's fine—I mean, I don't—" John coughed again. "Water?"

Constantius snapped his fingers, and the girl that had come into John's room earlier suddenly appeared holding a mug of fresh water. John gulped from it and regained his composure. "Sorry, must have gone down the wrong pipe." The girl smiled at him.

"You were about to tell me about your necklace."

"What about it?"

Constantius took a bite and stared at John. "Why does Lucius want it so badly? Today in the games, Lucius volunteered to fight a lion beside you—all, apparently, because he wanted your necklace. Why?"

John swallowed, though there was no food in his throat. "I—I don't know." John held up the pendant. "It was a gift from a friend who's dead now, so it's very precious to me."

Constantius leaned closer to John and took the pendant into his own hand. John backed his head away but there was nowhere to go. The emperor smelled of sweet perfume. "So Lucius thinks it valuable?"

John tried to play it off with a shrug. "I don't know. Maybe?" He pulled the necklace out of Constantius's grasp and tucked it into his shirt.

"And Lucius wishes to be rich?" Constantius said it like a question.

"Probably," John said. Then, nervous, he chuckled, "I mean, don't we all?"

"I am rich, but I can always be richer," Constantius said. "When we apprehended Lucius, I retrieved this jade amulet that he'd stolen and returned it to you. Should I instead have had it appraised for its true value?" He held out his hand.

John froze.

Constantius grinned. "Don't worry, John. You are

more valuable to me than any jewel."

"Is that why I'm a prisoner here?"

"I know you are a friend to the Alemanni," Constantius said, again pressing forward with his elbows on the table, his hands clasped in front of him. "I know they are near, in the forest. They sent a scout and I let him see that you are alive."

A scout from the Alemanni? He must have been sent by Crocus. Had he rescued Sarah and Aurora already? Thinking of Crocus reminded John of the mission. *Unite Constantius and Crocus.*

Constantius interrupted his thoughts. "I want to speak to the Alemanni commander. Who is he?"

"Alaric?"

"Alaric," Constantius repeated, nodding his approval.

"But there's another that might be more willing to listen."

"Oh, who might that be?"

"Crocus."

Constantius eyed him for a moment and then let one laugh slip. "Crocus? You two like Romulus and Remus, the brothers who founded Rome, trying to make a new empire for yourself?"

"You have to unite with Crocus," John said.

"So sure of yourself." Constantius cocked an eye. "Well, if you're right, then maybe you'll be even more influential than Romulus and Remus. But how can I trust Crocus? I know he wants revenge for his father at Lingones."

John's face must have revealed his surprise because Constantius grinned and said, "Oh yes, I know more about Crocus than you do, my boy. And do you know what *really* happened at Lingones?"

John waited, assuming this was a rhetorical question. After a few seconds of silence, Constantius staring at him patiently, John replied. "Crocus said the scar-faced Roman—I mean, Marcus, I think is his name—he killed Crocus's father."

"That is part of the story, it's true. But obviously he hasn't told you what happened before that. I was traveling with a small escort on a trade mission. We were ambushed by a group of Alemanni barbarians who had crossed the Rhine. They massacred my men. I barely escaped with my life to the nearby fort of Langres with the barbarians so close on my heels that the garrison didn't dare open the gate and instead hauled me over the fortification ramparts by rope!" He laughed. "As they tugged me up the wall, an arrow pierced my side." He opened his tunic slightly to show a purple wound like a fat spider with veins for legs.

"Then what?" John asked.

"Then we won." Constantius closed his tunic to hide the wound. "We always win, John. We dispatched scouts to the nearby forts. Reinforcements soon arrived to aid their emperor. Over six thousand Alemanni died that day. Among them, Crocus's father."

John exhaled a puff of breath.

Constantius finished his pork and set his utensils aside. John fidgeted in his chair, but he was so hungry that he kept eating. Constantius pointed again to John's necklace. "Your bulla reminds me of my son, Constantine, fighting in the East. I miss him dearly."

"You want your son back."

Constantius stood and walked to the window, his back to John. "I want to return to a Pax Romana—a Roman Peace, when for over two hundred years there were hardly any wars and trade was plentiful. I want that again for my empire and for my son, but I fear for his safety every day. We are in the midst of a clash of cultures like none I've ever seen. There are Franks to the west, Goths to the east, Alemanni to the north. And now there is internal strife too. Diocletian has ordered that all Christians are to be fed to the lions, Romans or not. These are too many fronts on which to battle, and we are spread too thin. I fear for Gaul, and beware the fall of this region for our empire as a whole. I fear for my son's future."

Constantius turned and opened his hand to reveal a gold medallion. He flipped it through the air and John caught it. It was just like the gold coin he'd seen in the museum, with *redditor lucis aeternae* around the edge. He hadn't been able to hold the sample in the museum, and the thick medallion had a nice heft to it. This piece would certainly look nice in his coin collection.

"Restorer of the eternal light, John. That is what I aim to be."

John remembered that phrase as the translation of the Latin on the coin. He'd wondered before what it meant, but now he had the amazing opportunity to actually ask. "What does that mean?"

"The Franks bring nothing but darkness and doom from the west. Our troops have had a terrible time beating them. I believe that if we join with the Alemanni, together we can defeat our common enemy and restore light to the people. To all peoples of Gaul. That is why I want to speak with the Alemanni man who can make a decision to bond with my forces and end the threat of the Franks. Are you certain that would be Crocus, not Alaric?"

"It has to be," John said. In order to fulfill his mission, he had to sway Constantius toward partnering with Crocus. But would partnering with Alaric get the same effect?

"Well, then"—Constantius held up his wine goblet for a toast—"to Rome!"

John clinked his mug and they both drank. Constantius ordered the slave girl to bring out the dessert. A minute later she arrived with a silver platter.

"Libum cheesecakes, Caesar," she said, presenting the browned bun-size delicacies. Warm honey dripped from the sides.

His mouth full of cake, John asked, "So when do we leave?"

"Leave?"

"To deliver the message to Crocus."

"I am the caesar of Gaul, John. They come to me."

CHAPTER THIRTY-ONE

Dangling

JOHN

After dinner, John returned to his room, escorted by a new guard. The soldier closed John's door, but John didn't hear his footsteps leaving. John was a prisoner.

He walked to the window and looked out at the stars like jewels pinned to black felt. The air was crisp and clean and he took a deep breath of it.

His gaze turned down from his third-story window. Below him was a red-tiled roof that sloped toward an enclosed rectangular courtyard. Two floors below that was a large garden. If he jumped to the roof, he'd surely go rolling and sliding down into the open courtyard and probably break his legs. That wouldn't help anyone. But why escape? It seemed like he was on the path to uniting Constantius and Crocus.

He needed to warn his sister. If the scout knew he was here and reported that back to Alaric, wouldn't the Alemanni come in fighting? There would be a lot of bloodshed. Sarah could be in danger, right along with Crocus, Aurora, and the rest of them.

But if he could get to them first and talk with Crocus, convince them that Constantius was not a threat, maybe—

John paced. He couldn't leave out the front door with the guard there.

The slave girl's smile at dinner flashed into his mind. Maybe she would help him.

John chuckled under his breath. Was he seriously considering how he could escape the compound of the emperor of Gaul? He could imagine his report for fifth grade this year:

How I Spent My Summer by John Tidewell.

He had to find Sarah, unite Constantius and Crocus, then get Sarah to the arena to teleport them back home. Oh, and beware the man named Alex. No problem.

He slumped onto the bed and wrapped his hand in the sheets. His fist clenched the fabric, and he wanted to pound the mattress while tears of frustration threatened to pop from his eye sockets.

John smashed his face into the mattress filled with soft wool and screamed. Sometimes that helped. The bed muffled his cry, but there was an immediate knock on the door.

"Quiet down in there." It was the guard.

John sucked in his breath and was silent, but he pulled the sheet with both hands and all his strength, needing an outlet for his angst. With a fistful of cloth in each hand, he pulled with all his might, trying to tear it. It stretched taut in front of him like a rope.

Like a rope.

John looked to the window again. He played out the sheet in his hand. There was enough, tied to the foot of the bed frame, to lower him to the red tiles of the roof below.

Without a second thought, he swung his leg out the window. A chill breeze ruffled his hair and he shivered, but the cold wasn't the only reason.

John shook like the time he'd ridden in a glider with his dad. You look up and see the engineless plane coasting on the wind, and it looks so peaceful from afar, but inside it vibrated and jostled and lurched with the tide of the invisible currents. The constant roar of the wind inside that flimsy cockpit didn't let him think straight. That was how John felt now: anyone looking at him from the outside would have no idea the whirlwind going on within.

He looked down the steep pitch of the tile roof to the courtyard below, then lowered himself flat against the tiles. The incline threatened to pull him down, and he hesitated in letting go of the sheet.

Voices. Was the guard checking on him in his room?

No, they were underneath him on the second-story walkway directly below. Their voices echoed around the rectangular space of the courtyard and garden.

John remained still. He felt momentarily like Spider-Man. The theme song playing in his mind matched the rhythm of the heartbeat in his ears.

When the voices faded away, he slowly let himself inch down the roof.

He peered over the edge two stories down into an open-air garden, walled in on all sides. The moon lit the area, but there was no sign of any guards.

"Does whatever a spider can," he whispered the song anxiously, trying to distract himself from the height.

The second story below had a wide stone railing. A pot where flowers may once have bloomed sat near one of the pillars holding up the roof.

Fortunately, the pillar was carved with an ornate curving vine with plenty of footholds and handholds for a person of his size.

Just don't look down.

John swung a foot over the edge and felt for a place to support his weight. Finally it found a hold, and he lowered himself cautiously, his hands still on the edge of the roof.

Squatting, his right hand found a stone leaf that provided a good grip. He moved his right leg down, then his left. Good. Almost there. His left hand let go of the roof and grasped at the rounded pillar, hurrying to find a notch to grab. His fingers shook.

There. He got it.

Then he made the mistake of looking down, and his body tensed against the cold stone.

It's not that *far*, he told himself. *But probably enough to break your legs. Does this count as rock climbing in the Alps?*

He swallowed, clinging to the pillar with all of his strength.

Suddenly the stone in his left hand broke off and his torso went flailing out over the void. His legs still clung to the column. He yipped but his body tensed so quickly that it cut off a full-fledged cry for help. The bit of stone shot like a missile into the grass of the garden below him.

Adrenaline kicked him into action, and he swung himself back to safety, grabbed another handhold farther down, then quickly finished the descent to the second-floor hallway.

His legs wobbly, he lowered himself to a crouched position and leaned his head back against the railing while he caught his breath.

Then he heard a *psst* from down in the courtyard.

Oh no. They heard me.

John turned his head to look through the white stone balusters of the railing.

What looked like Alemanni fighters moved into the courtyard like quiet cats.

The hairs on his arm raised when he caught view of his sister.

Sarah, walking behind Crocus, next to Aurora. Alaric led the group.

They were here! He had to get to them. He had to tell them not to fight.

John's breath came quick as he scanned up and down the hallway. Empty.

Still crouching, he got on the balls of his feet and was about to show himself to Sarah when—

CHAPTER THIRTY-TWO

Betrayal

SARAH

Sarah wasn't *glad* to hear the noise of something falling into the courtyard, but it somehow felt better than the eerie quiet. Getting through the aqueduct and into the town had been too easy. They'd crept like ninjas into the villa of Constantius, but everyone was suspicious that they'd met no resistance. Still, they had to keep pressing forward.

That is why, when she heard something fall into the garden of the courtyard ahead of them, it meant that this villa wasn't entirely abandoned yet. And that meant John could still be here.

Sarah, Crocus, Aurora, Alaric, and the rest of the Alemanni tribe filed into the courtyard, weapons raised. Sarah could tell Crocus was growing impatient and wondered when he might just call out for the scar-faced Roman. As she pondered where that brute might be, Crocus's wish came true.

The sudden pounding sound of marching armor-clad soldiers didn't surprise her. It had seemed only a matter of time.

Lamps whooshed to life, showing they were vastly outnumbered and surrounded. All hope seemed lost, but Alaric and his men held their weapons and growled. They wouldn't be taken so easily.

"Come on!" Alaric screamed at the nearest Roman. "Attack, you coward!"

The Roman soldiers held fast, shields and swords bobbing in anticipation of defensive moves.

"Show me Marcus!" Crocus barked.

"I am Marcus." The scar-faced Roman stepped from behind the line of shields. "I should have killed you instead of just taking your hand at Langres. Come at me and I'll correct that mistake."

"Halt!" Constantius ordered, striding forward. "I told you not to harm them, Marcus."

Crocus curled his lip and strained against two Alemanni holding him back. Sarah knew that if he charged now, he'd be slaughtered. Maybe they would be anyway.

"These men killed some of my finest soldiers,"

Marcus pleaded to Constantius. "They deserve to die."

"And you killed my father while he was unarmed!" Crocus yelled. "You're a coward."

Marcus sneered. "You and I are the same, Crocus. We both want revenge."

Constantius walked over to Marcus and faced him eye-to-eye. "Back down, Marcus. That's an order."

Marcus gripped his sword with two hands but did not obey. "Caesar, please."

Constantius put his hand on Marcus's shoulder. "I'm sorry about your men, Marcus. But they are gone. And *these* men are our path forward to peace. I will only say it one more time: Back down."

Constantius turned to Crocus. "Join me." He looked to Alaric and the rest of the tribe and spoke loudly, firmly. "Join me to defeat our common enemy, the Franks. In return, I can guarantee your homeland north of the Rhine."

Marcus's jaw went slack. No one spoke. A torch popped.

"You mean to partner with these savages?" Marcus nearly spit the words.

"Be quiet, Marcus, or I'll have you in irons!" Constantius snapped. Marcus's head ticked back and forth, a scowl on his face, seemingly enraged at the public embarrassment.

Alaric stepped forward, glaring at Constantius. Two

Roman guards held up their swords to bar him from getting closer to their emperor, but Constantius waved them away. They hesitated, then obeyed.

"How can we trust you?" Alaric said.

"You are still alive, are you not?" Constantius gestured to the force he'd obviously prepared for this trap.

"And why shouldn't I just kill you now?" Alaric cocked his head back and scratched at the thick undergrowth of his beard.

Constantius stretched his thin-lipped smile. "Killing me will not stop the Roman Empire." He shot a glance at Marcus. "But join me against our mutual enemy, and we can return to a time of Pax Romana. I will guarantee your homeland."

Alaric spit on the ground at Constantius's feet. "You invaders called it peace, but you still murdered our people."

"You would leave us alone north of the Rhine?" Crocus asked. "And swear to it by your god Sol?"

Constantius nodded. "By the Unconquered Sun on this our holy day of Dies Natalis Solis Invicti." He bowed. "I swear it."

"Caesar, this is outrageous!" Marcus stormed over to the emperor and grabbed him by the shoulder. "You doom the empire."

"No, Marcus, this is our salvation, our path to light."

Marcus whipped his sword to Constantius's neck.

Sarah and Aurora gasped in unison.

"I've had enough of your speeches," Marcus said. "Forces march on your gates as we speak, and I have let them in. The Franks, led by Allectus. He is a better leader and more decisive in battle than you've ever been. He is better for the empire."

Based on how the weapons pointed, it was apparent that the bulk of Constantius's force was still loyal to Constantius. Marcus's men were outnumbered and suddenly flung their swords around, very skittish about the tense situation with their brothers-in-arms. Apparently Marcus had revealed his deceit too early, since Allectus and the Franks had not yet arrived.

Constantius looked genuinely surprised. "You've betrayed me for the usurper Allectus? This is treason, but what's more, it's madness. The Franks will not leave you in peace. Lower your weapon, and I may take mercy when considering your punishment."

A vague memory came to Sarah of hiding behind a boulder and listening to Marcus scold his flag bearer for mentioning Allectus as "our emperor." And it was clear that Marcus was now standing in the way of their quest to unite Constantius and Crocus. *Beware the man named Alex.* Was Marcus the Alex? Wait. Allectus. Could Allectus be Alex? If Lucas was called Lucius, would Alex be called Allectus? Certainly didn't seem like a leap in logic.

Sarah's attention was drawn to the hallway where the sound of a horse's hooves clattered on the stone.

"Hail Caesar Allectus!" Marcus called, still holding the sword to Constantius's throat.

A man with a virtual buzz cut, a mustache, and a tight breastplate rode into the courtyard. He grunted as he righted himself after ducking through the hallway, then surveyed the armies before him with a calm eye. He exuded military prowess. To each side of him were hardened warriors, clad in leather leggings, carrying oval shields with metal domes protruding from the middle. Many wore chain mail armor over their tunics, most with dull rounded helmets. Armed with a variety of swords, spears, and maces, they appeared to be a mishmash of mercenaries. This was not their first fight.

Allectus looked at his wrist. "Your hour has come, Constantius!" He laughed.

"Alex!" someone shouted. The man flinched as if he'd seen a ghost, then searched the crowd. Sarah recognized the voice right away.

"Who said that?" Allectus stood in his stirrups, much taller than when he was sitting down. "I have not heard that name in many years. Who called me Alex?"

That confirmed it. This man was Alex. She looked around for her brother. "John!"

John stood from behind the railing on the second-floor walkway and pointed. "Beware the man named Alex!"

"John!" Sarah yelled again, waving. He caught her movement and smiled.

"Crocus," John said. "You have to unite with Constantius. Don't you see it now? You have to unite to save your people!"

"Bowmen!" Marcus snapped. "Fire at that boy." A few of the soldiers hesitated, seemingly not seeing the danger from a ten-year-old boy. Others notched their arrows, following the order.

"Wait!" Allectus shouted.

"No!" Sarah cried as they loosed their first volley.

John ducked down as the arrows rained into the stone and the roof. A large red banner of the Roman eagle hung from the railing, and arrows sliced through the heavy fabric.

"You have to do something!" Sarah yelled to Crocus.

"John was right all along," Aurora said.

Crocus glared at Marcus, who had sided with Allectus, then finally at Constantius all alone. "Alemanni brothers! We side with Constantius to defeat the Franks!" He raised his sword and shouted a rallying cry. His tribesmen joined him, their voices carrying high into the night.

Constantius used the confusion to push Marcus's

sword away from his throat and draw his own weapon. Marcus swung hard. Constantius parried with the loud clang of steel on steel.

"Attack, you fools!" Marcus cried. His men cheered and fell into battle against the larger force of emperor Constantius.

Allectus ordered his Frankish soldiers to attack too. He did so calmly and sternly, no hint of emotion. "But I want that boy alive!" He pointed to the second floor where John had disappeared.

The Franks pushed into the fray against the Alemanni. It was pandemonium. Spears jabbed, swords slashed, the courtyard was crowded with men fighting for their lives and for their emperor, both of whom claimed the right to the leadership. This was an epic battle, and at close quarters, anything went. Fists, headbutts, knees, daggers. Sarah saw one man's nose break when a shield smashed into it.

Sarah ducked a sword, then dodged an arcing shield. No one was coming after her directly, since she posed no threat, but the tumult of the battle threatened her all the same. An Alemanni backed up suddenly in his fight with a Frankish soldier, knocking Sarah to the ground. She crawled on all fours quickly away from their stomping feet, then looked up for John, but there was no sign of him. She hoped with all her might that he wasn't lying in the hallway up there full of arrows.

Crocus swung his sword and hacked into the shield of a Frank trying to pin him against a column. The much larger man had the advantage and Crocus needed help. Sarah kicked the Frank in the groin, and he squealed. Crocus finished him.

"You saved me there, thanks!"

"I owed you one for pulling me up from that cliff."

"Watch out!" A spear sliced in between them, and Crocus brought his sword down into the shaft, breaking the tip and turning it into simply a big stick. The splintered end stabbed again, and Crocus knocked it away with his shield.

"This way!" Aurora called. She was behind a bush against the wall, hidden from the clash.

"Go," Crocus said to Sarah, turning back into the battle. "I'm going to find Marcus."

"He's over there!" Aurora pointed. "Fighting Constantius." Sarah could see their swords clattering together, each man straining to gain the advantage. Constantius seemed the weaker adversary, and he'd soon be bested.

Crocus sliced, dodged, and weaved through the fight. Marcus knocked Constantius to the ground and was about to skewer him with his blade, but Crocus threw up his own sword to block the killing thrust, saving the emperor.

"You!" Marcus sneered.

"Me," Crocus replied. Constantius rolled out of harm's way.

Marcus rotated his blade, and Crocus's sword nearly launched out of his hand, then he rammed his forehead into Crocus's face, and the boy staggered backward. They were nearly the same height, but Marcus was thicker.

"He's no match," Sarah whispered, losing hope.

"Crocus can handle himself in a fight," Aurora assured her.

Crocus curled his lip and charged, his sword held over his head like a lightning bolt ready to strike. Marcus parried in one swooping move. Sparks lit their faces. Crocus lunged again and Marcus jumped back, evading the wild swing. Crocus screamed, spittle flying from his mouth.

Alaric made a move toward Crocus, but the Frankish mercenaries stymied his progress. They pushed and shoved, but eventually Alaric beat them all.

As the Franks fell, Sarah realized that there were now more of the Alemanni and soldiers of Constantius still standing compared to the diminishing forces of Allectus and Marcus. The usurper Allectus didn't look nervous—Sarah doubted he ever looked nervous—but she could tell he was unhappy, perhaps even contemplating a retreat. He took his anger out through his sword, chopping into an Alemanni.

Crocus swung his sword, but Marcus countered. Crocus swung yet again, his knot of hair bobbing wildly. He swiped like a madman. Marcus dodged the blade—once, twice, three times—then knocked Crocus on the back with the hilt of his sword, sending Crocus to all fours.

Sarah jumped from her hiding place. Aurora grabbed at her and missed. One of Marcus's soldiers put out both hands to scoop her up, but she stomped on the insole of his foot. While he hopped on one leg with his head bent over, she twisted his helmet down over his eyes. He toppled into another soldier, and they both tumbled into the bush next to Aurora.

As they scuffled to regain their footing, Aurora bopped at both of them with a mace, then ran to catch up with Sarah.

There were even fewer men standing now. Sarah had to step over wounded and unconscious fighters strewn over the courtyard garden. A Frank and an Alemanni locked in a wrestling match both seemed exhausted, each trying to outlast the other while getting in a gut shot or a knee jab.

"Sarah!" It was John. She looked up toward the voice and couldn't believe what she was seeing.

CHAPTER THIRTY-THREE

Sacrifice and Mercy

JOHN

With jerky starts and stops, John used the banner to rappel from the second story down into the garden.

The battle had thinned out enough now that he thought he could descend with a relative chance of success. Success meaning "not killed."

Just past the first floor and heading steadily toward the ground, John heard the fabric rip. "Uh-oh."

He crashed onto the lawn. His elbow hit at an awkward angle, sending electric bolts into his arm.

"Not funny," he said while rubbing his funny bone.

He rolled over and saw Sarah pushing her way through the crowd toward him, eyes as wide as they could be, her head swiveling on the lookout for a swinging sword or falling ax that might stop her from her path to John.

A Roman fell in front of her and she leapt over him.

"John!"

"Sarah!"

John fell toward her with his arms out for a hug, but Sarah pushed his shoulders and flung him backward into the hallway just as the whoosh of steel whisked between them. She roared like a momma bear at the attacking Frank, which caught him off guard and made him stagger backward, apparently not familiar with the wrath of a preteen on the battlefield.

Sarah ran into the hallway and bumped back against the wall next to John. Aurora dove down next to them. The Frank regained his wits and approached with his teeth bared in a growl. An Alemanni struck his club onto the head of the Frank, making him go cross-eyed and fall in a heap. The Alemanni howled like a wolf, the furs over his shoulders rippling.

Sarah hugged her brother. He hugged her back. She smelled of sweat, but he was glad to hold her. For a moment, he closed his eyes with his arms around her. When he opened them again, Aurora was watching them with a sad smile.

"Is Crocus—" John didn't want to finish the sentence. Was Crocus dead?

A spear smashed into the brick above John's head.

Rock splinters peppered down on him.

"You!" It was Allectus shouting and pointing his stained sword toward John. "You're trapped in time too, aren't you?"

John had a hunch this was coming. When Allectus had looked at his wrist earlier and made a joke about the time, John knew a joke about a wristwatch wasn't something that someone from this era would understand.

As bad a guy as Allectus seemed to be, John felt a twinge of sorrow for the man. How long had he been trapped here? He'd said years? Who was he, really?

"I'll be back for you!" Allectus shouted at them. He cut at one of Constantius's legionaries reaching for him. Another legionary tried to grab the reins of the horse, but it bucked and kicked the man over. "Franks, retreat!"

"Let them go!" Constantius ordered, clutching at a wound on his arm. "But not the traitor Marcus. First, we will get our house in order."

Crocus and Marcus were still whirling at each other. The clang of their swords was the only battle that still reverberated through the courtyard.

John, Sarah, and Aurora ran to join the ring of soldiers watching the fight.

"Constantius, shall we intervene?" one soldier asked.

"Stay away!" Crocus snapped. His shoulders hung over, he staggered around, his words almost a slur. "This is my fight to finish."

"Crocus." Sarah put her hand to her mouth.

Marcus grinned slightly while stepping around the circle, tossing his sword from one hand to the other. He didn't seem as exhausted as Crocus.

Alaric put a filthy hand on Sarah's shoulder. "Let him avenge his father."

Sarah reached her hands to John and Aurora on either side of her. John remembered when she'd swatted his hand away only a few days ago. He squeezed and she squeezed back.

Marcus lunged. John twitched with the sudden movement. Crocus came to life and parried, then countered and drew his blade along Marcus's ribs under his arm. The man cringed and grunted, spinning away from the fight and walking the circle with his arm clenched tight against his side.

Marcus leapt after Crocus again, this time with an overhead chop. Crocus held his shield aloft to absorb the brunt of the force. The shield cracked and Sarah gasped. Marcus chopped again, two-handed, the wood splintering further, knocking Crocus to his knees.

As Marcus raised his arms for another blow, Crocus dropped his sword, drew his dagger, and plunged it into Marcus's thigh. The sword still came down onto

Crocus, but the power had been drained from the attack, and the blade glanced off what was left of Crocus's shield. Marcus's sword thunked into the earth. Crocus grabbed a mace from the ground nearby, jumped to his feet, and slammed the blunt weapon into Marcus's blade. It snapped in half. Unarmed and off balance, Marcus reeled, stumbling backward. He fell and clutched at his leg, the dagger still sticking out.

The crowd hushed.

Crocus shook off the useless shield from his stump forearm. He stood over Marcus with the heavy mace held in his hand.

John knew that one strike would crush the man's skull. He held his breath.

"The story of Fenrir is ultimately a story of sacrifice and mercy," Crocus said. He dropped the mace and turned to the crowd. "Týr didn't slay the wolf who bit off his hand; he contained him." He looked at Sarah, then at John and Aurora. "Marcus should be jailed for the rest of his days."

Constantius broke the eerie silence. "So says Crocus and so it shall be!"

Crocus turned from his fallen enemy and started to walk away when Marcus suddenly picked up his half sword and was on his feet, the broken blade plunging toward Crocus's back.

"Crocus!" Alaric burst into the ring and dove at

Marcus. The dagger in his hand flashed as he tackled Marcus to the ground, saving Crocus.

Crocus spun. Marcus stood up, but Alaric did not.

The sword had sunk into Alaric's chest to the hilt and he lay dying. Aurora ran and slid next to him. Crocus charged toward Marcus, but before he reached the traitor the man looked down at a dagger stuck in his ribs, then collapsed.

In a moment, both Alaric and Marcus were gone.

Aurora howled and buried her face next to her uncle's. Crocus stood still, staring at Alaric. A tear fell from his cheek.

The Alemanni hung their heads.

John hugged his sister. She pulled him close and led him away from the ring of Alemanni surrounding their fallen leader.

Crocus and Aurora held each other tight.

"Sorry about Alaric," John said.

Aurora nodded, sniffling, her eyes red.

Sarah let go of John and put her arms around Crocus. He hesitated, then his one hand reached to her back and held her firmly against him. They stood like that for the space of a few breaths.

When they let go, Sarah smiled and he smiled back.

"Thank you," Crocus said.

"For what?" Sarah asked.

"For saving my life in that battle, for one." Crocus smirked. "But also for reminding me about mercy when you saved that wolf pup. I shall lead with that sort of kindness in my heart." He took her hand in his and held it against his chest.

Constantius appeared, interrupting the tender moment. He put his hand on Crocus's shoulder. "I'm sorry for Alaric's death. I am. But *you* are the future of your people, Crocus. We worked well together to win this battle, and though we hurt him for now, the usurper Allectus will not stop. All he thirsts for is power and dominance over others. With your help, we will stop him. Will you join me to bring peace?"

Crocus looked over at John. John nodded with a grin.

Constantius held out his hand. Crocus clasped it in agreement, then Constantius held their hands in the air, as if declaring victory for a boxer in the ring. "For Rome, Gaul, and Alemannia!"

Near them, Alemanni and Romans alike cheered at the union.

John leaned to Sarah. "Guess our mission is done here."

Sarah nodded. "Yeah." She hesitated, her eyes locked on Crocus. "I guess it is."

"You're leaving now," Aurora said. "Aren't you?"

"Týr was wise to send you." Crocus clapped John on the back and then put his hand to Sarah's cheek.

"It's time for us to go home," John replied. He thought of his parents, likely worried in the museum with the chaos of the fire alarm.

Sarah sighed and glanced down at the pendant.

"I know the way," John said. "We have to go back to the arena."

Sarah cocked her head in surprise like a puppy who'd heard the keyword "walk."

Aurora hugged John. "I'm going to see to Alaric, but goodbye, John. I'm glad we met."

"I'm glad too," John replied. "Thank you for everything."

Aurora moved to Sarah and hugged her too. "Goodbye, Sarah."

"Maybe we'll see each other again someday." Sarah looked up to Crocus.

"I'd like that," Crocus said.

John and Sarah turned to leave. They didn't speak to each other as they left the villa of Caesar Constantius and walked up the road toward the arena.

Passing the gladiator school, they heard the distinct booming voice of Lucius coming from behind a barred window. The soft glow of a lamp shone from within. Was he singing?

"Shh," Sarah said. "Listen."

Just then, Lucius's face appeared at the window, and he stared up at the crescent moon.

"We can't just leave him in history," John said.

"Who's there?" Lucius asked. He looked around until he caught sight of John and Sarah. "Hey!"

"Why not?" Sarah asked. "He was in prison before too. And he tried to steal the necklace, John. We can't trust him." She shot him the evil eye.

"I guess," John replied.

"I promise," Lucius said. "I won't hurt you. I won't steal the necklace, either. I swear."

John looked at Sarah.

"No way!" Sarah said.

Lucius grabbed hold of the bars in his window and shook them with all his strength. The mortar of the window frame cracked as he roared.

"See!" Sarah yelled, taking a step back, pulling John.

"I want to be free!" Lucius yelled. He stopped rattling his cage. "But if I can't be, then I'd rather die here than that boring prison back home. At least as a gladiator I get paid and have a *chance* at winning my freedom." He scowled at them for a moment, and then his head disappeared from the window.

John and Sarah looked at each other. Lucius started singing again. "Swing Low, Sweet Chariot." His voice resonated deep on the *loooow*.

John and Sarah moved away briskly, casting a glance back over their shoulder occasionally as if Lucius would burst through the wall of his cell like the Hulk.

"I wonder about Allectus too," John said. "Shouldn't we try to save him? He's trapped here too, Sarah."

"That I really don't understand." Sarah scratched under her tangled hair. John explained how he'd been tipped off when the man looked at his wrist for a watch.

"Aten has some explaining to do," John said. "But should we try to find Allectus?" He asked it with an upturned eyebrow because the idea of running away from the arena and the portal home, out into the wild to chase an enemy of Constantius and Crocus—it sounded ludicrous.

"We can't save everyone," Sarah said. "That wasn't the quest."

"Right. The mission." John accepted that reasoning. They'd already finished the mission. His finger was itching to trace the eye of Ra.

"John, I want you to know I'm sorry."

"For what?" He shot his sister a side-eyed glance.

"For getting us into this. And for treating you so badly since we moved to Maryland. Well, really, since the trip to Egypt. I just felt guilty about dragging you into that mess and—"

John stopped and looked at his sister. "It's not your

fault. I thought you were mad at me."

"No, I'm not mad at you." Sarah grinned.

They walked a few more paces until they reached the crest of the seating for the arena sunk into the earth.

"We're a good team," John said.

"True." She smiled. "And this has been—well, quite the adventure." Sarah pretended to swing a sword at John. He parried. "But how do we get home? You said you know the way? For real?"

"There." John pointed to the center of the arena. The hyena snapping its crooked teeth flashed into his mind, but he blinked it away. He wondered what had become of Silko.

"The arena?" Sarah asked.

"We just need to be in the same location as where we arrived. The portal doesn't move. Like a tunnel or a gate. You arrive and you leave through the same gate." John pointed again to the center of the ring.

"How do you know?"

"I don't know. But I'm right, I felt it. And think about it: When we went to ancient Egypt, we arrived in the step pyramid in Saqqara in that tunnel, right? And when we escaped, we—"

"Traced the eye in the tunnel. In the same spot where we'd landed." Sarah's eyes lit up. "Of course! It's so simple. Wait, didn't we trace the eye when we first arrived in the arena?"

"You did, but not in the same spot. Remember? You were about to trace it, then Crocus pulled me away from the fight between Lucius and the legionaries. We didn't try again until we were there." He pointed to the arched hallway where they'd escaped the arena on that first day in Aventicum. "Crocus may have saved our lives and got us stuck here at the same time."

"How do you know all this?"

"I don't know how," John said. "But I know there's only one way to find out."

They both ran down the stone steps of the arena, hopped down the wall into the sand, and sprinted directly into the center of the ring.

An electric thrill tingled John's skin. This was it. This *had* to be it.

Please, please, please, please.

He held the pendant with surprisingly steady hands while tracing the almond-shaped eye, then over the line with the curlicue finish. As his finger moved down the line with the knifelike edge, John closed his eyes.

CHAPTER THIRTY-FOUR

Home Again, Home Again

SARAH

Sarah knew it had worked before she even opened her eyes. Along with the bright flash, she'd never been so happy to hear a fire alarm. It was blaring the same as when they'd left the museum. Wait, since it was the same moment as when they'd left—Sarah opened her eyes to see Aten waking in the corner, shaking his head and massaging his temples.

"Sarah!" John beamed, hugging her tight. "It worked! We're home!"

"Aten," Sarah said, pointing. She wanted to ask him so many questions.

Aten leaned into a sitting position. He was wounded from his fight with Lucius—while he was still Lucas—

but the old man was stronger than they'd given him credit for originally. Aten scanned them up and down. "You did it. You traveled through time." He smiled. "Now you understand."

"No," Sarah snapped. She stomped over and stood above him. "I don't understand. How did you know about Crocus? And Constantius?"

"I told you. I am the gods' messenger." Aten wasn't speaking sense. "You will have more errands like this. To save the world from—"

"Grave danger, yeah, you said that. But what does that mean?"

The fire alarm silenced. Aten looked around.

John tugged on Sarah's sleeve. "Let's go find Mom and Dad."

"I want more answers," Sarah said, but the thought of a hug from Mom and Dad sounded like heaven.

"We'll see each other again," Aten said. "The gods have decreed it!"

Sarah backed away from Aten, John pulling her along. She wanted to know so much more, but right now she was tired and needed a break. A *real* break this time.

They joined a few other stragglers heading down the stairs toward the main exit. Since the fire alarm had stopped, people didn't seem as worried any longer.

"Weird," John said. "I wonder what Aten was

talking about. More errands? Does that mean we'll have more missions?" He sounded eager for the possibility.

"So we're time warriors now?" Sarah joked. "I want nothing to do with that guy." Then she pointed at the pendant. "Or that necklace. Dump it in that trash can and let's be rid of it."

John started to take the leather strap from around his neck as they walked, but he paused.

"What are you groaning about?" Sarah asked as they reached the bottom floor. The exit doors were in sight.

"I think—I think I'll just keep it a little longer," John said. "You know—for safekeeping."

"No way! Get rid of that thing before we get trapped somewhere else, like"—she saw a display for an upcoming exhibit on the ancient Aztec—"like there." She pointed at the picture of Tenochtitlan with a sign that said "Coming soon!"

John wrapped the pendant in his fist. "It seems too precious a thing, Sarah. I mean, what if we really are supposed to—you know, save the world." He snorted.

Sarah reached for the necklace, and John turned so violently, knocking her hand with his shoulder, that Sarah huffed.

John gritted his teeth. "Aten said the gods *chose* us, Sarah. There's obviously something going on here. Time travel doesn't just happen. We need to solve this."

She softened. "Together."

"Like we always do."

"Let's find Mom and Dad."

John tucked the pendant into his shirt.

Sarah wrapped her arm around her brother's shoulders as they opened the exit doors into a blast of sunshine.

CHAPTER THIRTY-FIVE

In the History Books

JOHN

The double hug John received from his parents felt better than a warm wool blanket during a snowstorm in the Alps. After worrying over what had happened to them during the fire alarm, their parents eyed John and Sarah strangely. Mom picked a twig from John's hair and tried to rub a dark smudge from Sarah's cheek. There was no explaining it, so they didn't try.

The next day, John brought his iPad into Sarah's room.

"Knock first!" she squealed, lying in bed with earbuds. She had her own tablet on her lap.

"Oh, sorry," he said. He had genuinely forgotten. "Look at—"

"I said, knock first," Sarah repeated.

John sighed, stepped backward while closing the door, then rapped his knuckles on the wood.

"Come in." Sarah sat up and took out her headphones.

He laid down his tablet open to a web page for coin collectors. "A coin just like this"—John held up the gold medallion Constantius had given to him—"was discovered by an amateur with a metal detector in March 2019 in Avenches, Switzerland."

"Neat," Sarah said.

He could tell she was trying to sound interested, but this is where he'd really hook her. "It sold at auction."

"Okay."

"For $552,000."

Sarah's eyes shot as big as golf balls and she choked. "What?!"

"Shhh," John said. "I don't want to tell Mom and Dad."

"Why?"

"Don't you think that would raise too many questions about our mission?"

Sarah tottered her head back and forth, considering the complications.

John tapped to the next tab on the iPad. "I searched for information about our friends."

"And?"

"Well, I couldn't find anything on Aurora. There are very few written records of the Alemanni people in general, so what happened to her is a mystery. Same with Silko. I'd like to believe he won his freedom, but that might be a stretch. I did find a mention of Lucius."

Sarah leaned in. "Wow."

"Yeah. Over a hundred fights as a gladiator and he won the majority of them. He even won his freedom several times but chose to stay in the ring. He eventually retired and lived to a ripe old age."

"That is not what I expected."

"The gladiator fights went on for another hundred years after we left," John said. "The last gladiator fight was in the year 404."

"Crocus stayed true to his promise," Sarah said, holding up her own tablet to show the same painting of Crocus they'd seen in the museum. He didn't look quite the same, but his pale blue eyes seemed to be following John. "Though he started out as an Alemanni who killed Romans, after he teamed up with Caesar Constantius they eventually brought down Allectus together. Maybe that's our 'why.'"

John flashed back to the parting sight of Crocus and Constantius arms up, side by side. "Why what?"

"Why was our quest to unite Constantius and Crocus? And why do you think Aten mentioned in the same sentence that we should beware of Alex?"

"You think that the gods wanted us to unite Constantius and Crocus so that they could defeat Alex together?"

Together. Silko's rallying words came back to John. *Together—that's how we'll get through this,* he'd said.

Sarah raised her eyebrows. "Something like that."

"Alex was interfering with the timeline of history. Our mission was to make it right." John's wheels were turning.

Sarah continued, "It's also written that Crocus was present when Constantius lay dying in Britannia and swayed Constantius to name his son Constantine as the successor for emperor. And we all know what an impact that was on history."

"We do?"

Sarah chuckled. "Google it."

"There's one more thing I want to show you," John said. He flipped his iPad to show his sister the photo of a rescue dog, all black except for a white splotch between its eyes. "We could name it Fenrir."

"Or—" Sarah grinned. "Mercy."

CHAPTER THIRTY-SIX

Back at the Table

SARAH

That night, sitting together around their family dinner table, Sarah took another forkful of the libum that John had prepared—with some help from their mom—and pushed it through the warm honey on her plate.

"Way better than hardtack," she joked to John. He giggled.

"I was considering marmot for dinner," John said.

Sarah laughed at that, though she had to admit the mountain critter wasn't half-bad.

John fidgeted with the eye of Ra pendant under his *Star Wars* Chewbacca shirt.

"I think we should go back," he said. "To the museum." He continued to play with the necklace.

"When the time is right, Johnny." Sarah glared.

"How will we know when that is?" John asked.

Her parents looked at each other, then at Sarah. Dad spoke first. "I thought it was a very well done exhibit. Can I start calling you *Filius* Invictus, John? You're my little Unconquered *Son*." He reached over and shook John's shoulder.

Sarah groaned at the dad joke, but she loved it.

"What's one thing you learned, Sarah?" Mom asked.

Sarah paused, images playing in her mind: Crocus charging into the magistrate's villa to save Aurora despite the danger to himself, how wholeheartedly he had protected that girl; how Crocus had risked his own life to save hers when she'd fallen over the cliff; the mercy he'd shown to Marcus. "Non nobis solum."

"What?" Dad asked.

"Non nobis solum," she repeated. "It means 'Not for ourselves alone' in Latin." She smiled at John.

"Huh," Mom said, eyebrows arched.

"Non nobis solum, I like it." Dad grabbed a second helping of the libum cheesecake and drizzled honey over the top. "And I love this dessert."

Sarah stood up from the table and rinsed her dish.

"One thing I learned . . ." John teased.

"Yes?" Mom asked.

"Sarah is *really* good with puppies."

Sarah giggled. "Yeah, about getting a dog . . ."

Libum (Sweet Cheesecake)

8 ounces ricotta cheese
1 cup plain, all-purpose flour
1 egg, beaten
bay leaves
1/2 cup clear honey

Heat the oven to 425°F and grease a baking tray. Beat the cheese in a mixing bowl and stir it into the flour along with the egg. Divide the soft dough into 4 buns and place on the baking tray with a bay leaf underneath each. Cover the cakes with a small overturned bowl and bake for 35–40 minutes until golden brown. Warm the honey and place the warm cakes in it so that they absorb it. Allow to stand 30 minutes before serving.

Source: https://bit.ly/libum-cheesecake

AUTHOR'S NOTE: FACT OR FICTION?

Warning: Spoilers ahead!

As I'm reading an intriguing historical adventure novel, it makes me want to do my own research on the topic. How much is true? How much did the author invent? After all, history is ripe with facts stranger than fiction, and, conversely, there are plenty of holes in the story of our humanity prime for the whims of an author.

I hope I've piqued that interest in you and while I don't want to turn this section into a research paper or Wikipedia page, I do want to touch on a few of the events in *Sol Invictus*.

First, I want to start with Crocus, since he was somewhat the impetus for the overarching story. He seems to have been a real person, but the times he lived in vary depending on the expert. There seems to be a general consensus and written record that he was a "king" of the Alemanni (in Roman terms) and also that he was a general in Constantius's army who counseled the caesar to name his son Constantine as the heir to the seat of emperor. I thought this conflict highly intriguing! Many of the tales of Crocus describe how he plundered the Roman settlements and created general havoc. But then later he sides with his enemy? Why? What was his motivation? That's where the history books lack specifics, and the author is free to take speculative liberties—that's where all the fun of writing comes out. On that note, there is no evidence that Crocus had only one hand. That was an artistic addition (or subtraction, as it were).

Regarding the gladiator "games," there is ample information on this topic I won't rehash. But I thought the story of the *bestiarii*, those condemned to the ring with the "beasts," was especially intriguing and disheartening. Some criminals were sentenced to death and cast into the arena with no weapons against fierce predators, while others—the venatores—fought the animals repeatedly and earned fame and fortune for their prowess and daring. Not all the animals were predators. These hunters displayed their skill against deer, wild goats, dogs, and rabbits, though the plethora of exotic animals is astounding. I have not exaggerated by including a rhino, hyenas, and a lion. There were fights with bears, tigers, elephants, crocodiles, jaguars, hippopotamuses, anything the local editor could get his hands on to amuse and excite the people. In the early second century, one emperor celebrated his victories at war through games reportedly involving 10,000 gladiators and 11,000 animals over 123 days. We think elephants are treated poorly in circuses now, but during the reign of Augustus Caesar, apparently 3,500 elephants died. It's hard to imagine.

In terms of female gladiators, a law passed in 200 CE outlawed freeborn women from participating in the games, indicating that before that there in fact had been female gladiators. Note that female slaves were still allowed to fight. How common this was is a point of scholarly debate.

Another point of debate is what is meant by "a turn of the thumb." I left it vague in the story, since there is no definitive proof that the editor turned his thumb down for an execution or up to save the life. In fact, many believe the opposite was more likely. Experts believe that the thumb turning down as a signal for death was only introduced in 1872 through a popular painting by French history painter Jean-Léon Gérôme entitled *Pollice Verso*. Before that, it may have been a common snub to flip your upturned thumb at someone (as it is still in many countries of the Middle East), and thus a Roman editor may very well have given the thumbs-up to indicate death to the gladiator.

I liked the name Alaric, but he was not an Alemanni.

That name actually belongs to a king of the Visigoths who sacked Rome in 410 and played an important role in furthering the decline of the Roman Empire. I encourage you to read more about him.

Silko was a real Nubian king in the fifth century CE. Arakamani was also a Nubian king, though probably about eight hundred years before that. His history is foggier. The Kingdom of Kush and the city of Meroë were real places with fascinating stories.

Allectus was a real Roman usurper who allied with the Franks. Constantius was deployed to Gaul in part to put down the traitor, at which he succeeded. As political propaganda and in response to a coin that Allectus had produced, Constantius minted his own coin to proclaim himself the restorer of the eternal light. If you happen to find one of those coins today, you are indeed fortunate! "In March 2019, an ancient coin showing the head of Allectus was found in Dover by a 30-year old metal detectorist. The coin sold for £552,000 at an auction" (http://bit.ly/allectus-coin).

About the Author

Ben Gartner is the award-winning author of The Eye of Ra adventure series for middle graders. His books take readers for a thrilling ride, maybe even teaching them something in the meantime. Ben can be found living and writing near the mountains with his wife and two boys.

BenGartner.com
Twitter: @BGartnerWriting
Facebook: @BenGartnerAuthor
Instagram: @BGartnerWriting

Read the exciting series!

Made in the USA
Las Vegas, NV
26 November 2021

35346173R00177